The Grieving Woman

M.L. Lexi

Titles by M.L. Lexi

The Blind Woman
The Deceitful Woman
The Forgiving Woman
The Grieving Woman
The Guilty Woman
The Loyal Woman
The Noble Woman
The Resolute Woman
The Unfaithful Woman

The Farfalla Family Saga

The Determined Woman
The Persevering Woman
The Invincible Woman

The Fearless Woman Series

The Fearless Woman
The Naïve Woman

Copyright

To friends who stick by you
no matter what.

We're the authors of our own destiny

—M.L. Lexi

Chapter 1

TODAY WAS THE day.

For weeks, Coco plotted, planned, and lied to make today happen. Now that the day was here, she was regretting it. There are doors that, once opened, can't be closed again.

Tapping the cell phone alarm off, Coco rubbed exhaustion out of her eyes. She hadn't had a decent night's sleep in weeks, and last night was no exception. Sitting up in bed, Coco brought her knees up, pressed her face into them and took a moment to gather her thoughts. As much as she'd mentally prepared for today, she wasn't ready. She felt the knot of nerves in her stomach wind tight.

Coco took a deep inhale. "What have I gotten myself into, Fredo?" Fredo looked at her, brown eyes dripping with affection. She rubbed his ears and kissed his head. "You're a great listener. If only you could talk." She pushed her tired body out of bed, walked to the bathroom, and stepped under the spray of hot water to wash the tension away.

It didn't help.

Coco's hair and body wrapped in Egyptian cotton, she walked past the luxurious creams pioneered by the Swiss dermatologists she worshipped and touted their benefit to her fans for years.

The daily hour-long skin hydrating ritual she'd religiously performed since she could remember seemed futile now. The same went for the five-mile runs to keep her tall body trim and shapely and everything she took to heart to keep her vanity and ego gratified.

Perfection was her trademark, her brand, had been since her teens. Now "was," was the operative word.

Everything Coco valued seemed trivial now, but when you were handed life-altering news, priorities changed.

Taking a slow, contemplative look at herself in the mirror, Coco saw the rich green eyes the camera loved shadowed with worry, but she wouldn't bother with make-up. Coco wouldn't bother blow-drying the mink-coloured hair featured in the L'Oréal commercials women envied and spent thousands of dollars to mimic.

Towel drying her hair, Coco haphazardly bundled it into a wet ponytail and walked to her closet. Eyeing the hundreds of designer outfits and shoes she'd collected over the years, she opted for the Dolce & Gabbana jeans, a Chanel silk blouse, and the Manolo Blahnik black patent flats. Some of her glamorous image had to be upheld, she thought.

"Come on, Fredo, let's go get me some caffeine and you breakfast." Coco shrugged into her leather jacket and opened the front door. The air that hit her had a fall chill to it.

Stepping onto her front steps, she hugged her back for warmth and filled her lungs with cool air. It was six a.m., and the world was hushed with dawn, dreamlike. Coco feasted on the green, rolling hills that spread to the horizon. She thought that in her trek around the globe, she'd never seen anything more beautiful.

In the east, framing the landscape, a round, yellow sun arising for the day lit the outgoing dark sky. Trees clad in scarlet and gold painted the escarpment. High above her, Canada geese flew in V formation, their honks amplified by the peaceful silence.

Following the stone path that led to the resort, fallen leaves thickly carpeting the ground crunched at her feet. Coco smelled fall in the soft wind that ruffled the lingering leaves on trees that rose majestically toward the sky.

Fredo dashed ahead of Coco, and she watched him chase after a squirrel who easily outmaneuvered him by jutting up an elm tree.

"Come on, Fredo. Both you and I know you're not climbing that tree," Coco called out. Seeing the logic in that, Fredo gave the squired one last "we'll meet again" stare and darted toward Coco.

The walk from her home to the resort was a short ten minutes but invigorating.

Reaching the resort's back terrace, she climbed the stairs. Chairs were tilted against the round teak tables to ensure rain drained off, their padding stored for the winter. The colourful pumpkin-orange umbrellas, which shaded their occupants from the sun in the summer months, were collapsed and secured.

Coco waved at the four guests adventurous enough to be up this early. They warmed up in hoodies, tights, and running shoes to get their daily run in before the hiking trail filled up. Most of the resort's guests found comfort in the warmth of their beds until late morning and preferred to enjoy breakfast in the indoor dining room in front of the crackling fire in the hearth.

"Straight to the laundry room for your breakfast, Fredo. Don't you dare go into the kitchen and get in Chef's way, or you'll become today's lunch special," she said before opening the door.

In the pristine kitchen, Chef and her crew were busy with the breakfast preparation. Blenders whirred, juicers squeezed, freshly picked eggs sizzled in pans and knives chopped. The air was scented with baking bread, brewing Toraja Sulawesi coffee, and everything healthy the guests of Covington Spa expected during their ten-thousand-dollar three-day stay.

As steep as the price was, there was an eight-month wait for the privileged and bragging rights for the stay. That had come about from Coco's marketing ingenuity.

Those privileged enough to land on Covington Spa's guest list ranged from dignitaries to high-profile celebrities looking for a few days away from the spotlight. The spa provided guests anonymity, peace and quiet away from the flashing lights, the paparazzi, and fans for the duration of their stay.

Skirting Chef whom Coco didn't dare disturb with idle morning greetings or chitchat—one of Chef's kitchen rules you observed if you cherished your hearing—she crossed to the coffeemaker. Coco reached for the pot resting on the hot plate and filled her cup with steaming, black coffee. In complete silence, Coco walked past Chef through the sliding doors and onto the terrace.

Sipping coffee, Coco felt the wave of fatigue wash over her. She hadn't slept a wink in anticipation of what was coming. Since concocting the plan to deceive Emma and Mary into the reunion at the spa, Coco's nerves were wound as tight as a spring. Her heart hitched at the deception, but there was no way around it.

She'd made the wrong choice for what she thought was the right reason. The consequence of that mistake forced her to fade overnight from her two best friends' lives.

She hadn't contacted them in ten years, and that was deliberate, but she needed them now because those she'd considered friends, when push came to shove, turned out to be profiteers. The people in her life were in it to exploit her for who she was and her money.

Mary and Emma never would. They were stay-with friends. The type she could turn to no matter the hurt she'd caused.

There was pain, a terrible pain radiating out from Coco's chest, and she rubbed the heel of her hand against her breastbone to smooth it out. Blinking back the tears, she prayed things went her way today. Emma and Mary were the only friends she had left and her last recourse.

DR. MARY CARTER-TYRELL WASN'T UP for the spa weekend her husband, unexpectedly, surprised her with. She'd rather spend the three days at a medical conference furthering her intellect to benefit her intellect and patients rather than her vanity. Not to mention, the one-hour she spent driving to the luxurious spa was time from her life she'd never get back.

Her husband, however, thought otherwise and threatened divorce unless Mary took the weekend respite seriously.

"Pfft, as if you'll find anyone better than me," Mary pointed out to her husband of fifteen years.

"I won't. It's why I need you to take care of yourself. You need the time off. You're wound tight right now, Mary. If you don't do it for yourself, do it for me. I don't want my wife suffering a myocardial infarction."

Mary's frown turned to a grin. Her husband knew medical speak made her heart flutter, and she conceded. "Fine. I'll go."

Adam pressed his mouth to hers. "Good. The relaxing spa weekend will keep hypertension at bay and ensure your systolic and diastolic rates remain at ideal levels."

At that, Mary threw back her head and laughed.

FROM THE GRAVEL DRIVE, EMMA LOOKED around. The gentle roll of green hills dotted with wild purple Salvia. The pageant of autumn colour painted the trees bordering the property and the gardens hemming the house.

The air was ripe with the sounds and scents of rural life. Emma smelled pine, hay, horses, and the freshness brought on by green country living. She heard the bubbling brook, the neighing of horses, the song of cicadas, the call of birds, and the quack of ducks. High above her, she watched the hawk, wings spread wide, as he glided in a staggeringly blue sky.

Emma was a city girl at heart, but she couldn't escape relishing the comforting, rural sounds.

Emma's eyes turned to the rustic but dignified, two-story brick house. Late morning sunlight gleamed off the tall windows accented by white shutters. There were colourful Muskoka chairs and a swing at each end of the wrap-around porch with a heritage railing. From the tongue & groove porch ceiling, hanging flower baskets overflowing with trailing lobelia and pansies dripped with colour. Purple, lemon yellow, and watermelon red chrysanthemums along the flagstone path winked up at the sun.

Emma could see a whitewashed barn encased by a wood fence just as she'd seen in the movies. She heard the muffled sounds of laughter from women mounting horses followed by thudding hooves on dirt.

A directional sign TO SPA pointed to a newer, modern-looking building of poured concrete, steel and glass. Through the sparkling glass, Emma could see an indoor pool with its glistening blue water. Loungers were filled with women lounging the day away. A whirlpool with a visibly rising hot mist overflowed with chatty women sipping tropical drinks with tiny colourful umbrellas.

Signs directed guests to a gym and a hot yoga studio. A salon offered hand and stone massages, mani and pedis, facials, and hairstyling. All the pampering to melt away tension was there for Emma to take advantage of for three glorious days.

Emma felt her tightly wound knot of nerves loosen.

Covington Spa, the chi-chi poo-poo health resort ninety minutes north of her downtown Toronto home that she'd never heard of, was what she needed.

The weekend getaway, courtesy of AZ Travel, which she'd never heard of and at first thought it to be a hoax, couldn't have come at a better time. Emma didn't remember entering any contest. Still, she wasn't about to pass up the luxurious spa weekend retreat. Life wasn't on her side—it never seemed to be—and she deserved a bit of pampering.

With her canvass carry-on in hand, Emma walked up the walkway and stepped onto the porch. Walking around, the brown-haired Chihuahua sprawled at the top of the steps, eyeing her with a raised eye, her hand dropped to the brass handle. She pushed the front door open. The warmth that came at her was as comforting as the homey interior she stepped into.

Sunlight spearing from the large window above the entry door dappled the lobby's flagstone floor. Wood-beamed ceilings roofed the tall foyer. Reclaimed pine flooring, the colour of honey, sparkled. The floating, winding staircase led to the guest rooms on the second floor. In the fireplace fashioned of river rock, bursts of sparks crackled maple wood and scented the air.

Checking in at the front desk, Emma was welcomed and directed to the living room to wait until her deluxe room was readied. With the thought of the luxurious holiday floating on the brain, Emma walked into the cozy living room with long, plush couches, comfortable side chairs, and thick rugs.

She came to a stop when she saw them. Momentarily frozen and dazed, it took Emma a moment to process.

Aside from the shooting sparks and hissing fire from the hearth, the only sound Emma heard was her unsteady breathing. It had been years since, without explanation, they'd disappeared from her life.

Coco looked every bit the glamorous celebrity she'd become and Mary, the respectable doctor she was. In worn jeans and a T-shirt, Emma supposed she looked every bit the unassuming cashier she was. Emma never felt as if she fit into their swank lifestyle, and today was no exception.

"Hi, Emma." Coco put a smile on her face, walked to her, and embraced her. Surprise coursing through her system, Emma didn't reciprocate. "Welcome to Covington Spa."

It took Emma a second to associate the Covington name. "You own this spa."

"Yes," Coco said. Her eyes levelled with Emma's now she added, "The free weekend getaway was a ruse to get you here."

"A ruse?" Emma stared blankly at Coco. "Why?"

"I'm wondering the same thing. Why did you feel the need to get Emma and me here on false pretense, Coco?" Mary returned stiffly.

Coco didn't make eye contact and said nothing, but dodging, after all, was her M.O., Mary thought. Instead, Mary and Emma watched Coco swoop to the bar and slop brandy into her glass. The shaking hand that made the ice in her glass rattle when she tossed the drink back made something cold skitter up Mary's back while Emma felt the pleasure of her luxurious weekend dim.

Part I

The Beginning

There is reason and purpose to many of the unforeseen events that crowd our lives.

—M.L. Lexi

Chapter 2

Fall 1972

THE ENTIRE SIXTH-grade classroom flicked eyes to the door when it swung open, and the plump, eleven-year-old stepped in. She wore a washed-out oversized red sweater, faded, baggy jeans, and scuffed Mary Jane flats. Her cheeks were flushed red with cold. Her Goodwill purchased plaid jacket was two sizes too big. When she removed her wool hat, her short, chestnut bob sprang to static attention.

Tamping back a smile, Mrs. Ellingham silenced the snickering children. When silence reigned, Mrs. Ellingham introduced Emma to the class as a transfer student from Holy Cross and signalled her to take the empty desk between Jane and Mary.

Feeling the thirty pair of eyes burning into her as she made the interminable walk to her desk, Emma caught her foot on Bobby's outstretched foot. Stumbling forward, Emma's lunch bag flew out of her hands before she fell hard against the tiled floor.

The snickers and laughter amplified and bounced in her head like a tennis ball. It felt like the taunts Emma endured for months at Holy Cross, which her mother hoped she'd escape by transferring to All Saints.

"A new start with new friends," her mother told her, and Emma now wondered if it was possible.

The glacial blue eyes that lifted from the tile floor to Mary's coal-black eyes were wounded and vulnerable. Mary responded to their plea. "Be quiet, all of you," Mary snapped at her cackling classmates. Sprinting to her feet, she helped Emma to hers.

"What's going on back there?" Mrs. Ellingham turned away from the blackboard to face the class, gone quiet.

"Just helping Emma to her desk, Mrs. Ellingham," Mary said as Jane gathered the spilled contents of Emma's lunch bag off the floor. "I'm Mary. This is Jane, my best friend."

"It's Coco." Jane's words came out slowly to ensure they sunk into Mary's head. "Try to remember. A brain the size of the universe, but she can't remember my name."

"Right," Mary said, rolling eyes to the sky. "She's suddenly decided to call herself Coco. Anyway, anyone bothers you, come to me. I'll deal with them." Mary circled a warning gaze around the room.

Not one to be left behind, Jane asserted, "Us, Mary. Us," she said, aiming a warning glare at Bobby and making him choke on the snorted giggle.

That was the beginning of a beautiful friendship. A new start with new friends, Emma thought.

Maybe her mother was right after all.

JANE, MARY, AND EMMA WERE AS different as three girls could be.

Mary was the smart one. She was medium height and lithe. The long-lashed charcoal-black eyes set in a heart-shaped face underscored intelligence. An only child of blue-collar parents, she had a caring, nurturing nature, which destined her to take care of the world.

Emma was the ordinary one. The baby fat she'd been unable to shed depleted her confidence and sense of worth. It defined her. She was the eldest of five. Her mother and father met at Bob's Supermarket, where they'd worked since their teens. As a deli counter slicer and produce stocker, they barely made ends meet.

Unlike Mary and Coco, Emma had few dreams and aspirations. She was a below-average student and awkward, but her heart was made of gold and as big as the universe.

Jane, or Coco as she now insisted on being called, was an average student, but she wasn't an ordinary girl. Coco was outgoing with a larger-than-life personality and beauty pageant good looks.

Her almond-shaped eyes were a rich green. She was tall, and at eleven years old, her body hinted at the stunning woman she was to become.

Coco's parents were killed in a car accident, leaving her an orphan as a toddler. She'd bounced from relative to relative until Aunt Abby rescued her. Aunt Abby—her mother's sister—took her in the day after she buried her miserable, drunken, children-hating husband of twenty years. With the miserable SOB dead and the life insurance windfall from the policy she took out behind his back deposited into her account, Aunt Abby filled her house with Coco's youthful laughter.

Coco became Aunt Abby's world, and she spoiled the girl whom she considered a daughter. Aunt Abby gave Coco the best money could buy. She gave Coco the liberties she never had growing up in a strict religious home.

Coco was taught to pursue her dreams no matter what barriers were put in her way. Aunt Abby drilled into Coco that the idea men were the intelligent, dominant sex was a myth propagated by men who realized women could easily gain power over them with sex.

When Coco's body burst from its teenage cocoon into womanhood, with the wisdom of experience and age, Aunt Abby saw what Coco couldn't.

Coco was a beautiful child, and she was becoming a stunning woman. The type of stunning men tripped over to be seen with. Her shiny, dark curls were as silky as her creamy, smooth skin. Long lashes haloed the jade-green eyes. Her legs were long and slender, and her sprouting breasts were perky and ample.

Secure in her awakening femininity, Coco handled herself with dramatic flair. Aunt Abby felt it was time to further her protégé's education on the art of male manipulation.

No man would manipulate or use her niece as her husband had her. Coco would not play subservient to any man, as the women in her family were taught. She wouldn't repeat her mama's mistakes. Coco would be her own woman and get what she wanted on her terms.

"A woman can get a man to do anything she wants. You are a woman and control the tide of your life as well as any man." Aunt Abby preached like a religious mantra. "I came by that information too late. Don't repeat my mistake," Aunt Abby said often enough until it was etched in Coco's memory.

Coco thrived being centre stage, and acting gave her that, and she told her aunt so. Coco confessed that her first taste of performing, at seven when she played Mary in the school Christmas play, stayed with her. But it didn't become a life's ambition until she saw Casablanca on the big screen.

The moment Ingrid Bergman sauntered onto the screen looking bigger than life, it was when Coco decided to become an actor. To grace the screen like Ingrid Bergman was what she needed to do.

Coco signed her name on a napkin and handed it to her aunt. "That will be worth a lot one day," she said with the determined look that told Aunt Abby it would be so.

As different as Coco was from Emma and Mary, as contrasting as their personalities were, and as much as they butted heads, it didn't colour their tight bond. The girls vowed they'd be best friends for life and stand by each other no matter what.

Emma, Mary, and Coco celebrated birthdays together. Holidays were spent at one another's house, and their families became intertwined. They spent weekends doing what girls do: talk about boys, mall shopping, pick out one another's clothes, do one another's hair, and learn the finer points of makeup application.

As the years passed, their friendship blossomed, as did their personalities—Coco's mainly.

Coco's beauty, her outgoing and charismatic persona made her the envy of every girl and the desire of every boy. It fueled her ego. Her need to be the center of attention intensified, as did her expectations. The world revolved around her.

Coco didn't understand Mary and Emma's practical nature or laissez-faire attitude. Mary's indifference to her appearance boggled Coco. There were days Mary wore the same outfit two days straight.

As for Emma's deliberate dismissal of her appearance, well, that bewildered Coco, who religiously dedicated an hour every morning getting ready for school and an hour at night on a moisturizing regimen.

At an early age, Aunt Abby drilled into Coco appearance equalled the level of success you attained and the quality of men you attracted.

And Coco certainly couldn't understand Mary's commitment to her studies. When did you have any use for science or complicated maths? Adding dollars and cents was simple enough.

But the culmination of a friendship that started years ago was set in stone and more important than anything. For the sake of friendship, Coco overlooked Mary and Emma's flaws.

Chapter 3

COCO, MARY, AND Emma crossed the road and together stood staring at the façade of MacKenzie High. Their first day of high school brought on a new phase of their lives.

The square three-story, red brick building with a flat roof and tons of windows was massive compared to *All Saints*. It reflected everything graceless of a mid-sixties structure.

In place of a schoolyard, there was a spread of grass dotted with tall elm trees and wood benches. In place of a schoolyard, there was a spread of grass with tall elm trees and wood benches. Groups of students milled about or spread out on the grass, talking or soaking the September sun. Young couples held hands, embraced, and kissed. From a car radio and someone's boombox, the Bee Gees, *Jive Talking* clashed with 10cc's *I'm Not In Love.*

It was high school. It was all so mature.

Coco, Mary, and Emma's heart pounded in their throat for very different reasons.

Coco might have been only fourteen, but she recognized the potential to meet her dream man increased exponentially. It was a treasure trove of men, not silly grade schoolboys, to dip into.

There were men of all hair colours and sizes. There were academic ones, athletic ones, and dangerous-looking ones, whom Coco eyed with interest.

Feeling as if she'd died and gone to heaven, Coco's eyes looked as if a spark had fanned to life in her.

For Mary, who'd hoped to enroll at one of the best schools in the city to allow her entry into a top medical school, she saw nothing but regret. Although the knowledge her blue-collar parents couldn't afford the private school of her dreams was real, it was nonetheless a disappointment to end up at the poorly rated MacKenzie High. She'd made do all her life, and she would do so now.

For Emma, fear was the single emotion coursing through her. High school was a big undertaking. She wasn't like Mary or Coco, who both knew what they wanted. She wasn't thin or beautiful like Coco, and she wasn't smart like Mary. She wasn't anything like the girls strutting their perfect bodies before her.

Emma was ordinary, and her confidence was as flat as her chest. She wanted to run away. The thought circled in her head until Coco slung an arm around Mary's and her shoulder.

"Ladies, let's get this party started," Coco said, smiling slyly.

The bubble of hysteria intensified in Emma. She didn't move. Instead, she brooded.

"What's wrong, Emma?" Mary said.

Calming Emma was as instinctive to Mary as impatience was to Coco, who rolled her eyes to the sky and thought that wasn't it just like Emma to hold them back. Timid Emma was always the downer, always the one to throw a wrench into an eventful situation.

"You can tell us anything," Mary said, casting a chastising look at Coco over Emma's shoulder.

"I wish I could feel as confident as you two." Emma hated sounding as foolish as she did. The moment, however, felt as stressful as the summers of her youth spent at *Heart Lake* when she was pressed by her parents to squeeze her plump body into a bathing suit. The dread that filled her then flooded her now. She wanted to be anywhere but there.

"Who says we're feeling confident?" Mary's voice rang with empathy.

"I am." Coco's dimples flashed at the muscular jock walking past them. She looked forward to finding out how he got the scar on the tip of his left eyebrow.

"Ignore her." Mary's elbow plowed into Coco's side.

"One, it's only high school. Two, we're here with you and for you, regardless of what Coco says. Understood?"

"I know, but I'm scared," Emma said quietly. "I don't fit here. You're the brainiac." She eyed Mary before she turned to Coco. "You're the beautiful one."

"I am that." Coco's comment netted her a second elbow to the rib from Mary.

"That makes me the simple, ugly duckling."

"I've told you never to describe yourself that way." As accurate as Mary thought, the statement was Emma wasn't going to benefit from drilling the negative thought into her head.

"It's true. Look at these girls." Emma watched the group of female students assembled at the school's entrance.

Voluptuous blonds, perky brunettes, sprightly red-heads wearing jeans a tad too tight, or skirts way too short skirts, ripe breasts spilling over sweaters hugged and bragged about their summer holiday. Many paraded their man. Arms tightly wrapped around them to claim ownership, they shot warning daggers to any girl considering muscling in.

"Sluts, all of them. They're what you call the go-to girls, not the stay-with girls. Look at how they're dressed," Coco said, with a dismissive wave of her hand. Eyeing Coco, in the tight pencil pants, white low-cut blouse, and polka-dot high heel sandals, Mary and Emma's eyebrows winged up. "What? I dress like this purely for marketing purposes. You never know when an acting scout is eyeing you."

"Right. Scouts. Here at MacKenzie High." Mary turned to Emma. "Everyone here is as scared as you are, Emma."

"You're not, and she sure as hell is not." Emma's eyes tilted to Coco, who was busy making eyes at the jock leaning against the elm tree.

Mary clamped a hand on Coco's arm, a warning to shut her mouth when she opened it. "Everyone here has their insecurities, even her."

"She's right." Coco pointed to her eyebrows. "They're too thin."

Mary's face creased in confusion. "What?"

"Thin eyebrows are a big deal for someone who wants to be on the big screen," Coco's eyebrows wiggle got the intended snort of laughter from Emma. "They're my Achilles' foot."

"I think it's Achilles' heel," Emma said.

"No, it's bigger than a heel. It's an Achilles' foot," said Coco.

Mary lifted a single dark eyebrow. "Right. Anyway, as I was saying, everyone has their insecurities. They hide it under a veneer of make-up or forged confidence or the fad of the week or...."

"We get it, Mary." Coco unwrapped a stick of Double Bubble gum and popped it into her mouth.

Mary dismissed the image of her hands wrapped around Coco's throat. "We'll always be here for you, Emma. You can always count on Achilles' foot and me."

"You can." Coco blew a pink-coloured bubble.

Emma tipped her head back so that she could study Mary and Coco's faces. There was a sweetness and a concern in their eyes that telegraphed they would always be the go-to friend she could turn to. It smoothed out Emma's anxiety. "You guys are the best friends a girl can have."

"We know." Coco sucked in the deflated bubble. "Now, let's get this party started." Coco slid an arm through the crook of Mary's.

"Well, are you coming, Emma?" Mary said, offering Emma her arm.

Taking a deep breath, Emma wiped her damp palms on her thighs. Sliding her hand through Mary's arm, she walked into the next phase of her life with her two best friends.

Chapter 4

STEVE JENKINS WAS a man who did things his way on his terms. Held back two years, he was older and wiser than most students of MacKenzie High—or so he told himself. The spill of long, dark, curling hair was as unruly as he was. His chiselled jaw was shadowed with a fashionable stubble. His customary attire of faded jeans, black T-shirt, and leather bomber jacket straining over broad shoulders topped the tough-guy look.

Steve Jenkins was the epitome of a bad boy. What woman didn't appreciate a dangerous man?

Steve pushed the door to the school cafeteria open. The air was crowded with the smells of fried potato, grilled hamburgers, cheap perfume, and teenage angst. Long Formica topped tables overflowed with hungry teenagers rattling on about their insignificant lives.

Eyes shielded behind mirrored sunglasses, Steve scanned the room, and like prairie dogs in the wild, every female head rose in unison. In breathless anticipation, they followed his every step wishing, hoping, praying he'd walk to their table. Shoulders hunched in disappointment when he walked past them.

Emma's stomach pitched and rolled when Steve headed toward her table. With a jolt, she sat up straight in her seat. Glacial blue eyes dripping with infatuation watched Steve slide his tall, muscular frame next to her.

Gog, he smelled heavenly.

Emma had fantasized about him for weeks. Many days, she watched him in silence, admiring the fit of his jeans. She imagined the arms with the long smooth line of muscling holding her and let her thoughts wander to what it would be like to lose her virginity to him.

With the studied cool of his twenty years on this earth, Steve eyed Emma. "Hey."

Emma evaporated.

"Hey." She swallowed heavily, her heart pounding with womanly longing.

"You're Emma."

He knew her name. Stunned silence followed. "Yeah. Sure. Mmm-hmm," she said when she found her voice. Emma's eyes trained around the cafeteria, pure feminine delight glowed in her blue eyes when she saw every girl eyeing her with envy. Her feathers spread proudly.

"I'm Steve." His breathy voice was like music to her.

The liquid warmth spread in her belly.

Yes, God, yes, I know. Did she bow to him? Did she offer her hand for him to pump? "Yeah. Sure. Mmm-hmm. This is my friend, Mary," she said, on impulse.

Never taking her eyes off her book, Mary gave him a hand wave.

"The studious one." Steve leaned closer to snatch a French fry from Emma's plate, and she breathed in the scent of sweat and man. It was the sweetest thing on earth.

Emma nodded. "She wants to become an OB/GYN. A doctor that deals with women's issues," Emma explained when his dark brows creased.

"Commendable, and what do you see in your future?"

Her heart did a quick gallop. He wanted to know about her. "I want to marry you and have lots of your babies," she wanted to say, but what came out was, "I'm not sure. I…." Emma stopped when Steve looked away from her to meet Coco's smiling eyes.

The plaid, pleated skirt, which rode high on her thighs, swung in tune with the graceful sway of her hips. She wore a pumpkin-orange blouse that accented the dark shock of hair tumbling down to her shoulders. Her lips were painted fire-red, and above the dramatic eyeliner, her eyes were dusted in copper.

Steve gobbled her up with his eyes. "Hi."

Steve hadn't looked at her that way, Emma thought, and for the first time in their friendship, she resented Coco. Emma seared her friend with a begrudging look, but Coco took no notice. Her eyes were coyly playing on Steve's male weakness.

"Thanks for waiting." Coco gave him a slow smile. "I'm done powdering my nose."

"A good powdering it was. You look great." Steve tucked his arm firmly around Coco's waist and pulled her in. "You ready to go?"

With a playful smile, Coco lifted a hand to push at her hair. "Show me the way, handsome. Thanks for keeping Steve company, Emma. I'll see you guys tomorrow."

"Later." Mary waved a hand without looking up, while Emma's resentful eyes followed Coco and Steve out the cafeteria door. "He's out of your league, Emma. A failed jock, who'll end up working construction." Mary flipped the page on her book.

"Your dad works construction," Emma snapped defensively and absently reached for a handful of French fries she stuffed in her mouth.

"Dad's an immigrant who didn't have the benefit of the education Steve's tossing out the window to work nights to pay for the spiffy Camaro and the designer clothes he thinks give him status."

It makes him look handsome and cool. "He's gorgeous, and I should have known better than to think he'd be interested in plain, fat me."

"Stop feeling sorry for yourself, Emma."

"Why is it so wrong to feel sorry for myself when everyone else has everything I want: looks, thin bodies, smarts, and boys?" Emma reached for the chocolate milk carton and drank deep.

"Because it serves no purpose to dwell in self-pity, and what I was going to point out is that he wasn't interested in me either."

"Yeah, but you have no interest in guys." Emma shoved hamburger into her mouth. "You're not a lesbian, are you, Mary?"

Mary stopped her drinking mid-sip. "Christ, Emma. Really?"

"I have nothing against it, but well, I never see you eyeing boys or hear you talk about them. And you don't express any interest in them."

"One, you know I'm focused on my studies. Two, no one at this school interests me. I'm what you call a sapiosexual."

"See, I knew it. Wait, what's a sap…?"

"Sapiosexual. It means I'm attracted to highly intelligent men, which we seem to be in short supply of around her. So, I'm waiting for medical school to scout for my man. He's going to be a doctor like me."

Christ, her aspirations were as ordinary as she was, as her life was, Emma thought. All she wanted was to marry and have babies.

"You need to focus more on your life, Emma."

"Yeah, maybe you're right, especially when Coco is a guy-magnet and every guy in the school is tripping over her. How can I compete with that?"

"She has no interest in any of them or Steve, for that matter," Mary informed her naïve friend. "Steve's arm candy, that's all."

Emma's hopes brightened. "You think."

"I don't think. I know. Unless Steve can get her on the big screen, she's not interested in anything other than to use him as a boy toy."

Good to know, Emma thought dreamily, tossing the last of her hamburger into her mouth. Maybe she had a chance with Steve when Coco sent him packing.

Chapter 5

STEVE WASN'T A passing ship in the night for Coco. Coco and Steve became an item—a four-year item.

As Mary intuitively concluded, Coco was in the relationship to fuel her ego. Steve, however, was too full of Coco to see that their relationship was a one-sided emotional affair. As Coco intended, Steve fell in love with her cover-girl face, her girlish laugh, her. She was in his head and blood. His thoughts revolved around her. He saw her in his dreams and craved for her when she wasn't with him.

The dangerous man became Coco's lap dog.

Coco's persistent demands didn't even daunt Steve. He didn't question her demand to be maintained in the unreasonable luxurious lifestyle. Instead, he dropped his factory job to work construction for more money.

Construction was hard, physical work, but the smile that came to Coco's face when he handed her the diamond bracelet or the Louis Vuitton handbag she'd always wanted was worth every backbreaking moment.

Steve was happy to give Coco everything she wanted and accepted the credit cards, the jewelry, and designer clothes without remorse. She deserved it. She could have the pick of any man in school, but she chose him and allowed him the privilege of introducing her as his girlfriend. Win-win, Coco reasoned. They both got what they wanted.

As a bonus, Steve was a great lover. Not that Coco had the basis for comparison or the benefit of feedback from Mary or Emma. Mary was saving herself for her Homosapien or something or other. As for Emma, well, she was Emma.

Coco had to admit Steve pushed all the right buttons. Steve made her body sing and drove her to the multiple orgasms she'd read about in Cosmo. Steve made every muscle in her body turn to water whenever he took her in the back seat of his Camaro. The sound of their bodies sliding over vinyl wasn't the most romantic, but when he feasted on her or pierced and filled her, there was no better feeling. That, in Coco's mind, was the definition of a good lover.

The fact Coco didn't love Steve was of no consequence when her needs were met. Nothing, however, stayed the same forever, no matter how much you'd like it to.

In a few weeks, they were going to graduate, and Steve was hinting at marriage. As if. Aside from the great sex, Coco saw no future with Steve. Besides, she was only eighteen years old with a dream to realize. She had her fame to achieve and her fortune to make. Come hell or high water Coco determined to see her face grace the screen.

Acting was in her system. It became more and more a part of Coco every time she stepped on the stage. From playing Mary in the Christmas play in grade three to Juliet in Romeo and Juliet her last year of high school and every play in between, acting dug its claws into Coco. It was deep in Coco's blood. Steve wasn't.

Coco didn't intend to chain herself into marriage and certainly not with Steve. Steve wasn't a part of her plans.

"Are you listening, babe?" Steve offered his cigarette, and Coco took it.

The scent of night flowing through the car window mingled with the smell of sex radiating from their body's around them. From the radio, Peter Cetera's voice flowed musically from the car radio to proclaim that if she left him, she'd take away the biggest part of him.

"Yeah, sure, I'm up for a movie tonight." Coco indulged in a quick drag while he slid his pants over his hips.

"Your mind's miles away." Steve stretched out on the back seat of the Camaro and spooned her naked body. "What are you thinking, babe?"

Coco turned the cigarette back to Steve. "I was just thinking how Mary made valedictorian." The glib lie slid off her tongue as her mind raced on how to break her news to Steve.

"She's a smart one." Steve took one last puff from the cigarette and flicked it out the window.

Coco felt his arms go around her, just below her bare breast. They felt strong and so comforting. She was going to miss that.

"She got into the University of Toronto, full scholarship. As for Emma...." Her mind wandered when she felt his fingers traced lightly over her nipples and left a wonderful, tingling feeling. "Christ, you have magical fingers."

A smile creased one corner of his mouth. He never tired of hearing Coco's approval of this male prowess. "I love exploring your body."

"Where was I?"

"Emma, something or other," Steve reminded, nibbling his way across her shoulders.

"Yeah, Emma. She's taken a full-time job at Bob's Supermarket for the summer. If I know Emma, that's where she's staying put. "

"What do you mean?" He moved his mouth to her neck.

"Just saying that's where we'll find her this summer and in years to come. Emma has no aspirations. She just wants to get married and have babies—lots of babies." Something Coco couldn't understand. There was so much she yearned to experience, so much she needed to do. Being tied down in marriage with the same man for years and motherhood wasn't on her bucket list.

"Family and children is not such a bad thing, is it?" Steve breathed in the smell of her hair. Lilac, he thought from the shampoo he bought her.

"It isn't if that's what you want." Coco sat up and reached for the black lace bra and shirt on the floorboard.

"And you don't want that." Steve watched her snap her bra close and thread her arms into the silk shirt. "You need to chase after this elusive dream of becoming a movie star."

Coco heard the ice in his tone, and she set her teeth against temper. She wasn't about to explain, for the umpteenth time, what he refused to accept.

He caught her arms before she started to jump into the front seat. "All I'm saying, babe, is that the movie business is tough. It's a one-in-a-million shot business."

"And you don't think I've got what it takes?" Coco froze Steve with her stare.

"You've got what it takes. I'm just worried they won't see it as clearly as I do." Steve pulled her into his arms, chained them tightly around her. "I don't want to see you hurt, baby. When you hurt, I hurt."

"I know. I'm sorry." Coco made herself smile.

Steve looked into the moss green eyes he'd fallen in love with. "Don't be. I'm only thinking of you."

"You're too good to me, baby."

Steve brushed the hair away from her face behind her shoulders. "I like taking care of you. It's why I want us to get married. I want to take care of you always, and I can. I mean, Mr. Edwards offered me the supervisor position at the site. It pays much more than I earn now. You know I'd never let you go without."

How could she tell him she was leaving for New York right after graduation? How could she explain she planned to break into Broadway, and from there, it was a matter of time before she made Hollywood her home?

Getting that much closer to what she'd dreamed about made her giddy with excitement.

"I don't mean to rush you, Coco. It's just that I love you so much."

Coco put her best performing face on. "I love you too, baby."

Chapter 6

WITH FAMILY, FRIENDS, and Steve looking handsome in the impeccably cut gray suit, blue silk shirt, and perfectly knotted tie, Coco, along with Emma and Mary, accepted her diploma. Afterward, Coco and Emma proudly listened to Mary's empowering commencement speech.

After the ceremony, Steve whisked Coco off to Cugino's for the surprise celebratory dinner he'd planned for days. For a short fifteen seconds, she considered turning the invitation down and telling him of her plans to leave for New York in the morning. In the end, Coco said nothing because no use spoiling a good dinner.

It shamed her for a moment, just a moment when after dinner, he helped her into the back seat of the stretch limousine, waiting to whisk them to the Royal York Hotel. Coco said nothing when Steve opened the door to the hotel room, and she saw the dozen white calla lilies—her favourite—spearing from the vase on the coffee table.

Coco held her flute out for Steve to fill when he popped the cork on the bottle of Dom Pérignon. The glass she lifted in salute stopped mid-air when Steve pulled out the velvet box from his jacket pocket and got down on one knee.

"Jesus, Steve." A spear of guilt sliced through the shock. Wide-eyed, Coco stared at the French cut diamond ring against black satin.

"I love you. I want you in my life. I need you in my life. Coco Smith, will you be my wife?"

Open-mouthed, she stared at him, the diamond, back at him. She'd hoped he wouldn't do this tonight. She looked at the diamond. The emotional whirlwind that slapped Coco in the face made her knees weak, and she fell back on the sofa.

They were passionate lovers for four years. Their physical relationship added a thrill and made the tedious years of high school bearable. But it was over now. She'd come of age and was ready to get on with her life.

"Steve...."

"I know you have plans. I want to be a part of them."

Coco had plans, so many plans. They didn't include Steve. She had a dream to fulfil, a career to pursue, and Steve wasn't conducive to realizing it. Being around someone with no prospects or goals other than work construction, marry and having children would weigh her down and hold her back. Besides, Steve wasn't one for the limelight. The limelight was all she'd ever wanted, and she'd do anything to get it.

Steve misread the regretful tear that spilled over and tracked a line down her cheek as impassioned heartfelt, and he said, "I know it's a lot to take in. You don't have to answer now, Coco. Just know I love you so much."

She gave him a hard, fierce hug. "I love you too," the lie slid off her tongue as she took his hand and led him to bed.

IN THE MORNING, COCO QUIETLY SLIPPED out of bed and gathered her clothes off the floor. With one last look at the sleeping Steve and the ring sitting on the night table, gleaming under the sprinkle of sunlight streaming through the window, she left.

COCO WAS UNUSUALLY QUIET ON THE ride to the bus terminal. She didn't share details of her night with Steve with Mary and Emma as she usually did. She certainly didn't tell them about the ring or proposal. Mary might understand her refusal to accept Steve's proposal. Emma wouldn't.

Emma was already piling on the guilt for leaving without telling him. Emma wouldn't understand Coco couldn't get herself tied down with someone like Steve, who again hadn't managed to graduate and was settling for a full-time construction job.

Emma wouldn't understand Coco couldn't saddle herself with a gaggle of whining, needy children into the domestic life Steve wanted. She was neither the domestic nor the motherly type. Coco wanted to live.

She didn't need the pressures of babysitting Steve.

The idea of leaving her familiar life and going at it alone in an unfamiliar city was overwhelming. And Christ, she was going to miss his talents in bed. The man was a sex God in bed. It was the only reason she'd kept him around for four years. But now, she had no intention of weighing herself down with Steve. Now was her time.

As much as Coco's mind weaved between doubt and uncertainty, the excitement she was getting that much closer to her dream was stronger than the fear. Blinking back the tears, Coco gave Emma and Mary a tight, bear hug before boarding the bus bound for New York.

Watery eyes cast out the bus window, Coco waved goodbye at Emma and Mary—at her old life. The next time she'd see her friends, she'd be a household name.

"How can she leave without saying goodbye to Steve? Because you know, she didn't. He'd be here to see her off if she had," Emma said when the bus rolled out of the station.

"You don't know that. Maybe he couldn't stand to say goodbye," Mary lied because she figured that was precisely what Coco had done.

Brow cocked Emma stared at Mary. "How could she do it? How could she hurt him like that, all to chase a dream?"

As much as Mary agreed that Coco was toying with Steve's emotions to chase at glitter and glory she might never find, it was her life to do with, as she wanted. As a dream chaser herself, Mary admired Coco's initiative and gumption and supported her. As her friend, she backed her all the way. It's what friends did.

"It's what she wants, Emma. Try to understand that."

"I understand her need to chase her dream, but to go off chasing something that may not happen in a foreign city on her own and leaving Steve and us behind is insane."

Mary bit back on enlightening Emma that she could never understand Coco's hunger to chase her dream over tying herself down and said, "She's not on her own. She's staying with my widowed aunt who's going to love the company."

"How you can be so casual about the way she's treated Steve is beyond me?" Emma skirted passengers trickling out from the Ottawa bus.

"We're her friends, Emma. We promised to support one another no matter what." Mary walked around the woman lugging a rolling suitcase in each hand while telling her two kids to keep up.

"You promised. I didn't." Emma's icy tone came through loud and clear over the announcement flowing from the overhead speakers. "She strung the guy along for four years. She took emotionally and financially from him."

"I know she did, and I don't condone it, but I can see things more rationally than you."

Emma stopped in her path. "What's that supposed to mean?" There was a snap in her voice.

Rounding the car to the driver's side, Mary aimed eyes at Emma over the roof of her Volkswagen Beetle. "You're in love with Steve. I'm not."

Emma's anger waned into a stunned look. "I am not in love with Steve."

"You are and have been since the first day of school when he walked past us. You've been good at hiding your feelings from Coco, but not me." Mary dug into her jacket pocket for her car key, thrust it into the lock. "We're a team, Emma. We support one another no matter what."

She huffed a breath. "Well, we can still express an opinion."

Mary slid into the driver's seat and reached to flick the lock on the passenger door. "It's not your place to judge, Emma. How would you like it if she passed judgement on your decision to opt-out of fostering your education over a paycheque?"

"We both know that's you talking. Cashier work is lowly for you. Well, for your information, my parents need financial help." Emma's lips closed into a long, firm line.

"Honest work is not lowly, and don't you think I know what it's like to be strapped for cash? My parents are the definition of cash-strapped. I just want to make sure it's what you want."

Biting on her lower lip, Emma aimed her eyes out the window. The sky was a bright summer blue, streaming sunlight. Emma watched people rushing to catch buses or greet arrivals. The air flowing through the opened car window smelled of diesel and the spicy scent of hotdogs oozing from the cart at the station's front. She suddenly craved a hotdog or two.

"I'm sorry. You know I don't aim or ask for much, and my parents need help. You and Coco are only children. My parents are looking after my sister, brothers, and me. That's six mouths to feed, and if I can help them, then cashier work is what I need to do. It's in my cards. We support one another no matter what." Emma reminded Mary.

Mary pressed her fingers to her eyes. "Of course we do."

Seeing the guilt in Mary's eyes, Emma said, "In my next life, I'm coming back as the queen of England," to infuse levity into the sober moment.

"Queening is not all it's cracked up to be. It's a restrictive lifestyle. Then there's that Phillip guy because you know there'll always be a Phillip whose bullshit you'll have to put up with." Mary flashed Emma a smile, and she mirrored it.

"I'm going to miss you, Mary, when you go off to university."

In a gesture of friendship, Mary reached out for Emma's hand, squeezed tight. "I'm not going off. U of T is downtown and…."

"You're going to be busy with your studies. Not that I don't want you to be, I mean, I can't wait to call you Dr. Carter." Mary let the sound of the words roll in her head. It was music to her ears. "But Coco's gone, and you're all I have."

"I will be swamped, but I'm always here for you."

"I know you will be, but everything's bound to change now. We're heading in our own directions, becoming adults, and it's unavoidable. Friendships break under the weight of change."

"Ours won't, and, Emma, I'm not the only person you have left. You have you. Believe in yourself, Emma. Do what makes you happy. Go after what you want. What you want." Mary hoped Emma understood the underlying meaning of her words. "That hotdog smell has made me hungry. Let's grab lunch."

"You read my stomach."

Chapter 7

Fall 2002

COCO OPENED THE cold box behind the bar, reached in for the bottle of Kristal, and waved it in the air. "I thought we could toast our reunion."

Mary aimed lit eyes at Coco. "Hard pass for me. What I'd like is an explanation as to why you've lured me, us, here, Coco."

The ice in Mary's tone and the heat flashing from her eyes had Emma falling back on the couch. Steering clear of the bloodbath that was about to follow when Mary and Coco's sharp tongues lashed out at one another was the smart move. She wasn't as strong as they were.

"I'm waiting, Coco." Mary folded her arms across her chest. "And remembered that bullshit you get away with men doesn't work with me." The words sharp and cold as a knife telegraphed Mary's cautioning to Coco loud and clear.

Nerves bouncing, the words trembling on Coco's tongue didn't come out when she opened her mouth. In one quick gesture, she tossed sparkling champagne back to wet the throat gone dry.

"What? No scripted dialogue, Coco?"

Coco had one, but she wasn't ready to recite it yet and based on the anger in Mary's tone, she wasn't open to hearing it. What Coco had to tell them had to be said at the right moment under the right circumstances. Now wasn't the time.

"Just as well. I can't imagine we want to hear anything you have to say. You made your choices, and now you have to live with the consequences of those choices."

"I want to hear her," Emma said softly. She hadn't meant to defy Mary, but the guilt for what she'd done to Coco stirred to the surface, and she felt she owed her that much. Besides, whatever was going on between them—and there was a lot there—didn't involve her. "We support one another no matter what." Emma reminded.

Mary laughed caustically. "She doesn't know the meaning of those words. Do you, Coco? I need air. I'm going for a walk," Mary said before storming out.

There were doors that, once closed, couldn't be opened without a lot of effort. Mary made that clear, Coco thought, tossing the remaining champagne in her glass back.

Mary could be hard, cold, and unforgiving, and she wasn't going to make it easy for Coco to do what she needed to do. Coco knew that well enough.

Mary hadn't made it easy for Coco when after reappearing in their lives after years of absence, she demanded Coco disappear in return for her silence. If Coco didn't play her cards right, if she didn't handle the situation correctly, Mary would turn Emma against her. Emma was impressionable and easily swayed by the strongest voice, and at that moment, Mary had the upper hand.

It was going to take a grand leap to gain Mary and Emma's trust back. Coco hoped when she told them what she had to, it would do the trick. If there was a time she needed them, it was now.

Chapter 8

EMMA WAS THE ideal employee. She was punctual, polite, and efficient. Her till was never short at the end of the day, and she always went the extra mile for customers. It wasn't long after she started working at Bob's Supermarket that Bob promoted her to head cashier with a pay raise. The raise was marginal, but the boost to Emma's confidence was significant.

For the first time, Emma felt her life had meaning and purpose.

Emma took her head cashier role seriously. She sold Bob on the idea of footing the bill for uniforms for the five cashiers. Uniforms, she told Bob, projected a professional appearance, identified the cashiers to customers, and promoted his brand.

Bob was so pleased with the polo shirt, khaki pants, and striped apron emblazoned with his logo, Emma designed, he put her in charge of outfitting all his employees.

Bob gushed with praise when Emma outfitted every department with its identifiable apron colours: green for produce, brown for meat, white for deli, wheat for bakery, and pink for the florist department.

Emma's ingenuity earned her a bonus. She never imagined anyone rewarding her or calling her creative, let alone rewarded for it. Emma's confidence soared.

Emma cashed her bonus cheque and headed straight to Mel's Hairdresser. She set a couple of bills on the counter and told Mel, a flamboyant hair artiste, to transform her.

"Oh, darling, it's going to take a lot more money than that pittance to do something with this," Mel said, running fingers through her dried, split end, hair never cut under anyone but her mother's hand.

"Is that any way to talk to a customer?"

Standing over her, Mel looked into the blue eyes in the mirror coming at him. "You didn't let me finish. I've watched you for years walk past my salon and have wanted to get my scissors on this mess years ago. As the artiste I am, I will do what's necessary. Now," he slid off the rubber band that bound her hair and let the chestnut mop fly free, "sit back, darling and watch Uncle Mel work his magic."

Two hours later, Emma's hair was honey-brown, mink-soft, and layered to suit her round face. Excited by the outcome of his artistry, Mel didn't stop there. He had his makeup artist teach Emma how to apply makeup.

That was the beginning of Emma's transformation.

Emma replaced her ill-fitting, dated wardrobe with a fresh look with the remainder of her bonus money. It wasn't easy with the limited funds, but she managed it by shopping at the vintage stores Mel recommended.

Baggy sweatshirts were replaced with colourful, second-hand designer dresses, skirts, blouses, and tank tops. Pencil-thin pants now hung in place of the worn, loose-fitting. Makeup lined her bureau.

Emma took Mel's recommendation and bought herself a sexy lace bra and matching panties. No one would see her in it anytime soon, but Mel said that feeling feminine was what she needed. Mel was right. The surge of femininity led Emma to undertake the challenge of shedding the baby fat that had dogged her into adulthood, and she joined a gym.

Emma's newfound confidence and transformation weren't enough to stop her nerves grinding when Steve walked up to her register to check out his purchase.

"Hey." Steve's voice made Emma's belly flutter as it always had, as it always would.

"Hi. Umm, can you slide your items closer, please?" Her voice trembled before she steadied it.

"Yeah, sure. Sorry for my messy appearance, but I've come straight from work," he said when the blue eyes studied him intently.

His bomber jacket and hair were covered in dust, and his pants were speckled with paint. There was visible dirt beneath his nails and around his cuticles. The dark hair was unruly, and his jaw shadowed by the day's growth of beard.

He looked good enough to eat, Emma thought. Every muscle in her body turned to water, and she said, "If you buy three of the canned Romano beans, you get fifteen cents off."

"Thanks, charge me for three. I'll grab the additional can on the way out."

"Okay. Sure. Beans are a good choice. Healthy," she prattled on.

"I don't know about that. For me, it's a quick, easy meal. Open, heat, and eat. Now that I'm living on my own, easy is what I need."

Emma marvelled at the news. "You're living on your own."

"You can call it that. I moved into my parents' basement. I'm fixing it up, still working on the kitchen, hence the selection of canned foods."

"Sounds exciting." She tucked a strand of hair behind her ear.

"You changed your hair, and … everything else. I like it." He noticed. For a full fifteen seconds, her keying fingers stopped mid-air on the register. "You look really good, Emma."

As much as the compliment delighted Emma, her cheeks took on a faint tint of pink. "Thank you."

"Have you heard from Coco?"

Her smile faded. "No. Not a word."

"You're not lying to me, are you, Emma?"

She lowered his eyes. "Of course not. Nothing's changed since the last"—few thousand—"times you asked me," she lied.

She and Mary spoke to Coco every Sunday. During their weekly call, Coco complained about everything and anything. New York was expensive, and she couldn't afford many things. Mary and Emma knew Coco's complaints had nothing to do with affordability and everything to do with the fact that ten months on, she'd been turned away at every audition.

During their conversations, Coco never asked about Steve. When Emma brought him up, Coco informed her, Steve was the past and that Hunter, Charles, Grant, or whomever the actor of the week who'd promised to get her a part in the play they performed was the now. Failure to fulfill their promise resulted in immediate replacement. And from the sound of it, there was no shortage of actors in New York.

"You're her best friend. You must know where she's at, where she's staying." Steve watched her bag the rest of his groceries without making eye contact. "I just want to make sure she's okay."

The gentleness of his voice smothered her with guilt, but she'd promised. We're a team, Emma. We support one another no matter what. Besides, how was she to tell Steve, Coco moved on with her life and wanted nothing to do with him?

"Wherever she is, I'm sure she's fine." Emma handed Steve the last bag. "Coco's a survivor."

She knew where Coco was. Steve saw it in her eyes.

"Are you busy this Saturday, Emma? Thought I could take you out for pizza," Steve said. The short interactions at the checkout counter hadn't gotten him anywhere. Maybe spending a couple of hours in an intimate setting, sharing a pizza, might entice Emma to be more forthcoming. "How does *Cugino's* sound?" Steve prodded her along when she remained staring.

"That's a ritzy place."

Coco's favourite. "A classy girl deserves to be taken to a ritzy place."

Her eyes widened. "You think I'm classy."

"I do."

"We can share a pizza or a lasagna or whatever you like. Talk some."

Her mouth opened in a stunned O. "You want to talk … to me."

"I do. I want to get to know you."

"Honey, accept Romeo's invitation already. My feet are killing me, and I gotta get home to the kids." Mrs.

Hayes impatiently pushed her piled groceries down the counter.

"I'm sorry for keeping you waiting, Mrs. Hayes." Emma handed Steve his receipt.

"No problem, honey." Mrs. Hayes turned to Steve. "Pick her up at six, Saturday. Be respectful and treat her like a lady. Now move along, Romeo."

Emma turned to Steve with a conceding smile. "What she said."

Chapter 9

EMMA MOVED BACK far enough, looked at herself in the round dresser mirror. Twisting and turning, she liked what she saw.

Looking at the way the long spill of curls fell around the face with eyes dusted in copper put a smile on her face. Her smile widened at the way the cherry-red painted lips looked thick and full. Bless Mel's talented makeup artist for teaching her the tricks of the trade.

For the first time in her life, Emma liked herself, and her confidence swelled. She made a mental note to buy a tall floor mirror. She'd be looking at herself more often.

Eyeing herself in the mirror, she smoothed the front of the black dress that clung perfectly around her slender curves and dipped in all the right places. The dress was more revealing than she was used to wearing. It was more of a Coco-style dress, but Emma was going on her dream date.

It shamed her into feeling as giddy as she did.

Emma studied her reflection in the mirror and saw the guilt in her eyes. It hadn't ebbed since she'd accepted Steve's invitation.

She should have followed her instincts and called Coco to get her blessing. Friends didn't date their friend's ex-boyfriends. An implicit sacred oath existed between friends, but she talked herself out each time Emma picked up the telephone to Coco.

By Emma's logic, Steve was only interested in extracting Coco's whereabouts from her. He wasn't interested in her, and their pizza date wouldn't go beyond tonight. Why bother Coco with trivial details?

Emma caught a glimpse of the photo tucked in the frame of the dresser mirror. Mary and Coco's tender smile didn't feel so tender. She felt Coco's eyes burn into her and Mary's pass judgement.

"Stop feeling guilty. It's just pizza between friends," Emma told her reflection. "Besides, you look too good to waste it in front of the television."

When the doorbell rang, Emma took one last look and turned to head downstairs. Halfway down the stairs, she paused when her sister opened the door and saw Steve.

He wore brown loafers, navy slacks, and an olive green leather jacket against a white linen shirt. His stubble was neatly trimmed, and his dark hair curled over the raised collar of his jacket. Emma felt her knees buckle and she remained cemented on the spot, watching Steve interact with her sister.

"Are you Steve?"

Steve aimed his trademark sassy smile at the eight-year-old girl with the flowing dark curls and probing cerulean eyes. "I am, and who are you, pretty lady?"

The glow of delight was swift on the girl's face. "I'm Maddie. I'm Emma's sister."

"Hello, Maddie. Are you coming with us on our date?"

Maddie let out a girlish giggle. "I'm only eight years old. I'm too young to go on a date, silly."

"Well, that's my loss. I'd be very proud to be seen with a girl as pretty as you."

"You would?"

"Definitely." Steve watched Maddie go thoughtful.

"You can ask me out for pizza in one year. I'll be in grade four." She held four fingers up. "I'm sure Mommy will let me go out to eat pizza with you then."

Steve's lips curved, he knelt in front of Maddie, so their eyes were levelled. "It's a date. Until then, a beautiful flower for a beautiful girl." The words said with such tenderness made love roll through Emma in one fast unrelenting wave to encompass her entirely. Emma didn't think it possible she could fall deeper in love with this man.

Emma watched Maddie's grin widen when Steve turned over the calla lily in his hand. She wondered if Steve realized the impact his words and action had on a young, impressionable girl. No matter the age, a girl never forgets the first compliment, and she certainly doesn't forget the first flower she receives from a man.

"Look what Steve gave me." Maddie proudly held the flower out to Emma.

"It's beautiful. If you put it in water, it'll keep for a while?" Emma said with a warm smile.

"Okay, I will."

"What do you say to Steve?"

Maddie turned. "Thank you for the flower, Steve."

Steve flicked a friendly finger on the tip of Maddie's nose. "You're most welcome, beautiful."

Maddie giggled. "Next time you want to eat pizza, mommy can make it for us. She makes the best pizza."

"I'll keep it in mind."

Emma patted Maddie's behind to send her on her way. "Go on. Get your flower in water. Ask Mom to help."

"Okay, Emma. Bye, Steve."

"Bye, beautiful." Steve and Emma watched Maddie skip her way to the kitchen.

"Thank you. That was a lovely thing you did for her."

"How could I not?" Steve reached for Emma's coat when she plucked it off the wall hook. "She's a cutie."

"Can't argue with you there." She threaded her arms into her jacket when he held it up.

"The flower was for you."

"I know." She walked past Steve when he opened the door and stepped through the doorway.

The evening air was cool on her face and ripe with the scents of spring. The ironwoods and sugar maples that lined the street showed new growth. The warm glow of pooling light from lampposts brought the street alive. Above, a round moon suspended in a dark sky shone brightly.

"You like children?" Emma said.

"I do. I plan to have a houseful."

"That's quite ambitious." Emma wondered if he'd shared that piece of information with Coco, who'd made her disinterest in motherhood clear from a young age. Coco theorized she wasn't a breeding machine and wouldn't enslave herself to a husband or children.

"What about you? Do you like children?"

"What do you think? I have four siblings, Maddie and triplets boys. For a while, I wanted to have a gaggle of children. Now though, two will suffice. I'm the one that's going to blow up like a balloon, and I'm not going back there again."

A smile moved across his handsome face as he opened the car door for her.

OVER THE STREAM OF ROCK AND roll music from the car radio, Steve and Emma's conversation on the drive to the restaurant ranged over a myriad of trivial topics. Emma hated the banality of their conversation, but she had to ease into the moment she still believed surreal.

Cugino's Ristorante was as classy as Coco described it the first time Steve took her. Waiters in white and black livery wound their way through the maze of tables to serve drinks in tall glasses and food in oversized dishes. At the centre of each table, a fresh red rose speared from Baccarat crystal. Dimmed lights and candles flickering on white linen tablecloths lent to a romantic atmosphere.

Emma smelled the rich scents of stone-oven pizza, sautéed garlic, and grilled meat. Over Dean's breathy vocal singing *That's Amore*, Emma heard the soft murmur of conversation between couples punctuated with laughter. She hoped that would be Steve and her by the end of the night.

Steve ordered a bottle of Chianti, a large Margherita pizza, and a family-size Mediterranean Salad to share— all of Coco's favourite dishes. "You're going to love the food."

"It smells great in here." Emma cringed the moment the words were out, but this was her first date, and she wasn't sure what passed for a proper conversation.

"By the way, you look great tonight, Emma."

The flush that rose to her cheeks pleased Steve. If there was one thing he did right, it was to flatter a woman. He hoped his suave tongue would break through the solid wall of friendship between Emma and Coco and get him answers by the end of their date. Steve had to find out where Coco was holed up. Once he did, he'd be off on the first flight, train, or bus out.

Steve blamed himself for Coco's abrupt departure. He realized now his proposal caught her off guard and made her panic. Steve couldn't blame Coco for reacting as she had. He should have handled it better.

He had months to think it through, to consider the angles, and all indications led to blindsiding Coco with the proposal. Steve saw that now and this time, when he found her, he'd give her the breathing room she wanted. He'd even support her crazy dream of acting. He'd do what Coco wanted and wait for as long as needed.

Still, he'd carry the ring with him for when the opportune moment arose. Coco was an impulsive woman. She'd say yes when he least expected it.

For now, he'd focus on Emma. Emma was the key to finding Coco. Emma was the key to his happiness.

"You like working at Bob's?" Steve set a slice of pizza on Emma's plate.

"I do. Bob's been good to me." She hummed at the first bite of pizza. "This tastes amazing. Not as good as my mother's, but it's good."

"I'm glad you like it." Steve picked up a slice for himself. "Did you know Bob's real name is Eustace?"

Emma almost choked on pizza. "Eustace, no way.

"Yes. I guess Bob's a step up the masculine ladder."

"You know I can't unhear this. Now every time I see him, I'm going to have to stifle the laugh. How do you know this?"

"He's my uncle through marriage once removed or something like that." Steve drank some wine and signalled for her to do the same. "The wine's good. Try it." He topped her glass when she drank and several times afterward, hoping to loosen her mind and lips.

Their evening went better than Steve cared to admit. Emma was interested in what he said. She listened intently to his work stories and laughed at his corny jokes. She even listened to his car talk without telling him her mind was going numb, as Coco so often did.

Emma was interested in him. *Him.* It felt good, and he let the unfamiliar feeling swamp him. The sensation washing over, he was sidetracked, and by the end of the night, he wasn't any wiser to Coco's whereabouts.

A second date was in the cards. Whether the date was for pleasure or information gathering purposes was up in the air.

Chapter 10

FROM THE STAGE, where Coco played the minor part in the off-off-Broadway play no one would remember, she spotted him sitting front row centre. How could she not? The overpowering force of his presence was hard to miss.

He wore a white silk shirt and perfectly knotted gray tie against an impeccably cut Italian suit that cost more than what she'd earned in the past three months. His skin was dusky gold from hours spent under the California sun. He had an aristocratic, straight nose, a perfectly chiselled jaw, and luscious, thick lips. His hair, gloriously wavy, was as black as onyx as were the eyes locked on her.

He was exotic looking and radiated the same smouldering sexuality in person as he did on the big screen. He was Carlo D'Onofrio, Hollywood royalty.

Coco read in the tabloids his parents emigrated from Italy without a penny to their name and settled in New York when Carlo was eight. The youngest of six, Carlo D'Onofrio, started modelling at a young age to help keep his large family fed. Carlo was thirty-seven, single, and über rich. To his surprise, he quickly became a brand in high demand.

Carlo's face was associated with commercials that sold hamburgers, potato chips, designer clothes, automobiles, and toothpaste. Working his way up from television advertising to the movies now made him a Hollywood icon.

In the past three years, he'd starred in four worldwide box office hits, generating millions of dollars in revenue. Influential directors such as Coppola and Spielberg sought Carlo and paid millions for the privilege of coupling their work with his name.

Coco had seen Carlo backstage a couple of days ago. Doing her homework—as she did with all her soon-to-be male interests—Coco marked him as the replacement to Jewel, her latest arm candy. Jewel, the man with the ostentatious name, became expendable when it became clear the off-off-Broadway gig on *I'm A Man* was the best he could do for her. A tree stump could do better than Jewel.

Almost one year on, and she'd managed to be hired twice, and both gigs were for plays as far off Broadway as it got, with a combined dialogue of six lines.

Carlo was older than she was, but sacrifices had to be made to move her career along.

Carlo believed in giving back to his hometown and community, and supporting the off-off-Broadway scene was his way. Carlo's patronage was prized, recognized, and prized by those who wouldn't otherwise get the opportunity to realize their dream. Known as Papa New York, he gave upcoming artists a leg-up regardless of skin colour or lifestyle.

As appreciated, as Carlo's generous endowment was, what everyone looked forward to his unpredicted visits were. Carlo's "pop-ins" to scout for actors, writers, and directors were legendary. The lucky chosen were whisked to Los Angeles, and on his recommendation, doors which otherwise would never be opened were.

When Coco found out Carlo's reason for being there, she made it a point to get his attention. One way or another, Carlo would know her. She'd make sure she made it to the top of his list.

From the stage, Coco gave Carlo a wink of pure mischief that got his attention. After the closing curtain, as planned, he came to her backstage with an outstretched hand. "Hello, I am Carlo D'Onofrio, Miss…."

Coco stifled the delighted smile and, in a sober tone, she said, "Coco. Just Coco, you know, like Cher."

Concluding Smith was too ordinary, and the reason she wasn't getting the roles she deserved, she jilted the surname like one of her lovers.

"Nice to meet you, Coco." Carlo's breathy voice laced with that underlying Italian accent he tossed in just because it made women swoon was music to her ears.

Coco's eyes fixed on him for a solid fifteen seconds before they widened in shock. "Oh my gosh, you're him." She pressed a hand to her mouth. "You're Carlo D'Onofrio. The Carlo D'Onofrio," She fanned herself with exaggerated gestures. Now he stifled a smile. "I'm a huge fan. I've watched every movie you've made. I know most of the dialogue for *The Fugitive*, which is my favourite movie of all time." She delivered the scripted response, meeting his hand and enveloping it between hers.

The girl needed a lot of work on her dramatic performance, but she was stunning, he thought and concluded the camera would love her.

"I'm humbled by your presence, Mr. D'Onofrio." Coco reached in to pick the stray lint on Carlo's lapel when a group of her cast members walked past. Appearances were crucial in this business.

"You're a good actor, Coco."

"Thank you, but as much as I've been told you are the master for recognizing talent, how can you tell? I was on stage for the whole of five minutes with three lines."

"Five minutes or one hour doesn't matter, Coco. It only takes a few seconds to make a lasting impression on your audience."

"And did I leave an impression on you, Mr. D'Onofrio?" Her voice took on a sensual purr.

"You did that, Coco. You're acting is as memorable as your beauty," he said, to stroke her ego. He knew women well, and the one before him was as vain as they came.

Her ego swelled, Coco tried her best to sound nonchalant. "Again, thank you, Mr. D'Onofrio. That is considering you rated me a good actor, not great."

"My friends call me Carlo, and I'm not talking about your stage performance. That requires a lot of professional training, but you have potential," he added, when her mouth rounded into a shocked O. "I'm talking about the performance you put on to get my attention and the one you're putting on now. It's award-winning."

The words were a punch to the stomach. Her jaw clenched. "Is that so?"

She wished now she'd never started the contact that led to this moment. It wasn't what she bargained for or needed. As right as Carlo might be, the truth wasn't what she wanted to hear. For her state of mind, circling reality was what she preferred.

Being around professional actors had opened Coco's eyes and made her realize she wasn't as talented as she'd alluded herself to believe. Coco also learned that life didn't give you what you wanted just because you wanted it. Twenty auditions later, and the best she could do was three lines in a sorry-ass play was proof. Now, hearing it said aloud, by Carlo D'Onofrio nonetheless, made it too real.

"I take it no one has dared to tell you the truth. How are you to improve without constructive criticism?" He watched her eyes cut away from his. He slid his fingers under her chin, pinching as he turned to face him. "I mean it when I say you have potential. What you need is to polish that potential with professional acting classes."

"I'll have you know I got every lead part in high school." Anger spit out of her eyes.

"Honey, this isn't high school."

Fury simmering, she barked, "No, it's worse. It's off-off-Broadway."

To think she'd put out to Jewel for the past three weeks. She wouldn't mind it as much if he were a good lover, but the man was a two-star at best. Their sexual encounters compelled her best-acting face and performance. It was at times like those she missed Steve the most. No one had topped his talents in bed.

"And don't call me honey," she barked.

She was a firecracker, he thought, biting back the smile she wouldn't appreciate and get him a fist to the face. "You sure as hell won't make it in this business with such thin skin."

"Sure. Yeah. Okay. Are you done because I am?" Don't cry, don't cry, don't cry, she repeated in her head. "I need to change into my street clothes," she said, gathering her props off the table. "You're lucky you're good-looking because your charm isn't your most valuable asset," she murmured, piling the gray wig, cape, and hat in her arms.

"See, that's constructive criticism, which I accept."

Huffing out a breath, Coco's eyes flashed up at Carlo like two flares before she stomped off.

The grin that curved Carlo's lips expressed amusement and admiration. She was feisty, the take-no-prisoners type. He liked that. And she sure as hell wouldn't put up with his shit. She was perfect.

"Have dinner with me." He called after her. Her face went brilliant with pleasure, but she didn't respond. "I'll wait for you in the limo upfront. Don't disappoint me."

COCO DIDN'T MEET CARLO. SHE SNUCK out of the theatre's back door and went home. If Aunt Abby taught Coco anything, it was that as a woman, she controlled the tide and always must. She might sleep around, but it was on her terms, not a man's.

Coco might not be as worldly as Carlo D'Onofrio, but she could see that his offer for dinner was a preface to the casting couch. Someone as arrogant as Carlo D'Onofrio had to be set in his place.

Chapter 11

IT WAS CARLO who set Coco in her place when the following day, expecting him to come crawling, she found out he'd left for California. Worse was that Carlo chose curvy, busty Milligan as the year's up-and-coming star. Rumour was she was slated to get a part in Carlo's upcoming movie.

It felt like a slap in the face to Coco—the second in under twenty-four hours.

First, the smug asshole tells her she can't act, effectively ending her dream, and then he dismisses her. The moment Coco found out he'd boarded his private jet and left, it was minutes before the curtain opened for the night, and she stormed out in temper.

No one rejected Coco.

The sensation of rejection remained strong in Coco for days. How dare Carlo tell her she had no talent and invite her to dinner in the same breath? And when she played hard-to-get—her right as a woman—he left. Any man worth their salt would have chased after her.

How dare he? No one did that to Coco.

She humiliated herself, and the sting of embarrassment had her wallowing in righteous anger. Rejection wasn't a feeling Coco was accustomed to nor liked. Nerves tightly coiled, Coco stalked around her bedroom.

"To hell with Carlo. I don't need him." Thoughts racing through her head, Coco fell back on her bed.

"Damn it. I need him. I need him more than he needs me."

The unfavourable outcome of her interaction with Carlo had Coco doubting everything Aunt Abby taught her, everything she believed in. Maybe, just maybe, Aunt Abby was wrong—about everything. Questioning herself was a first. It wasn't a good feeling.

The gnawing at her stomach getting the best of Coco, she reached up and into her top closet. Behind the shoebox, she found the stashed pack of cigarettes from her rebuking landlady. Mrs. Carter was as preachy and judgmental as her niece Mary was. Worse, Mrs. Carter was under the mistaken delusion Coco was the daughter she never had.

If Coco had a steady job and decent income, she'd pack up tomorrow and move to her own place. She had neither, and beggars couldn't be choosers.

Walking to the window, Coco slid it open, shook a cigarette out of the pack, and connected the lighter to the cigarette. Coco watched the exhaled smoke rise to an overcast sky. The air was heavy, and lead-gray clouds opened up to rain over the city. In an instant, dew skimmed over the ground and grass and hung from leaves.

Coco could see the first signs of Mrs. Carter's yellow and white tulips and purple asters, which would transform her small backyard into an oasis of colour bursting into bloom.

This was Coco's first spring in New York. As much as she'd come to love the rushed life of the city that never slept, she had to make her move to Los Angeles. It was clear Coco wasn't going to make it in New York.

Broadway wasn't her cup of tea, and maybe, just maybe, she might make it in L.A.

As much as Coco detested Carlo, he was the only person who dared tell her the truth. She needed someone like him to guide her. Carlo was her only chance at attaining her goal because, talent or not, she wasn't about to give up.

Carlo could open the doors she needed to be opened. He was a big-ticket name, a Hollywood legend, and she let him slip away because of her arrogance. Coco cursed Aunt Abby and her feminist views. Those views had worked fine with high school boys, but Carlo was a man of the world.

Coco pressed her fingers to her eyes. She'd made a fool of herself with Carlo. The thought washed over her like a cold shower.

"You idiot," she repeated, over and over. She needed a drink.

Flicking the cigarette out the window, Coco crossed to the bed. Reaching under her mattress, she felt her way to the bottle of cognac—another vice she kept hidden from Mrs. Carter.

The drink went down smoothly and untied some of the knots of her creation in her belly. After her second shot, control and common sense reigned and the idea formulated in Coco's head.

Walking to her dresser, Coco reached into the top drawer and fished out the Actors Guide. She might as well make use of the monthly union dues she paid.

Coco flipped through the pages in search of names of acting coaches. After some consideration, she picked Amy Ford. First thing Monday, she'd call her to discuss coaching lessons.

Fifty minutes and four shots later, Coco heard Mrs. Carter yahooing from the bottom of the stairs. "Coco, dear, would you come down here please," Mrs. Carter called out in her high-pitch piercing voice.

Coco opened her door an inch. "I'm a little bit busy, Mrs. Carter.

"You have a visitor, dear."

"I'm not expecting anyone."

"Well, he's here to see you."

"Please send them away, Mrs. Carter. I'm not in the mood to entertain anyone."

"Come down, Coco. You've been cooped up in your room for days, and I think you'll be interested in speaking with this visitor. I'll show him to the living room while you freshen up."

Coco pressed her fingers to her temples. "Fine, I'll be down in ten."

Thirty-five minutes later, Coco strolled into the living room, stopped when she saw the man sharing a cup of coffee with Mrs. Carter. She took a scan when she didn't recognize him.

He was strikingly handsome, with a thick wedge of black, short hair that crowned the dimpled face. His eyes, so green against the smooth, black skin in direct contrast to Mrs. Carter's pallid, wrinkled one, held a sexy, slumberous look. In the burgundy blazer and white crew-neck T-shirt, he looked casual and stylish. At five-eight, next to the petite, blue-haired Mrs. Carter, he looked like a giant.

"What did I tell you?" Mrs. Carter said as Coco's eyes, bright with alcohol, stared.

The man swallowed coffee before flashing an all-perfect-teeth smile. "When you're right, you're right, Mrs. C."

Coco narrowed her eyes. "Who's he, and what are you both talking about?"

"This is Alex, dear. He's a…."

Recognition setting in Coco cut Mrs. Carter off. "You've been at several of my performances, and I've seen you backstage talking to my castmates."

Alex nodded. "Guilty."

Her eyebrows shot up suspiciously. "Who are you? How do you know where I live?"

"Settle down, Coco. I was telling you that. Alex here is a…." Mrs. Carter blanked out. "Oh, dear, I've forgotten what you told me you do. You know my memory isn't what it used to be."

Alex patted Mrs. Carter's wrinkled hand. "A P.A., Mrs. C."

"Yes, that's it, a P.A." Mrs. Carter handed Coco the cup she filled with coffee. "Drink it. It'll sober you up."

Coco breathed for control. "I'm not drunk. He's a private dick?"

Mrs. Carter sent Coco an affectionate amused look. "You're three sheets to the wind."

"It's four sheets to the wind, Mrs. C." The man reached for a biscuit. "These are delicious."

Mrs. Carter's face beamed. "It's a family recipe. There's plenty more. Have as many as you like." Mrs. Carter turned to Coco. "You honestly don't think I know about the cognac bottle under your mattress. It's me who changes your bedsheets," she pointed out. "And I know about the cigarettes too."

"How could you possibly?" You old bat. "They're…."

"At the top of the closet, behind the shoe boxes," Mrs. Carter finished. "I do own a step ladder, and calling me names isn't helpful."

"I didn't say anything."

Mrs. Carter offered Alex a napkin. "She thinks I'm an old bat, nosy, and intrusive. The thought rolls around in her head all the time."

"How…? Anyway, I think the issue here is that you've been going through my things." Coco's glaring eyes stared.

Mrs. Carter lifted a bemused brow. "That's hardly the point. Anyway, just make sure you don't burn the house down. Now, sit, drink your coffee, and have a biscuit to fill your stomach. Go on. Sit." Eyes hard as stone told Coco she'd better do as told.

"Yes, ma'am." Coco slid into the couch next to the man.

"Now, this is Alex, and he's a P.A., which is a personal assistant. He's here to take you in that limousine parked out front to the airport where a private jet sent by Carlo D'Onofrio is waiting to whisk you off to Los Angeles."

There were times the old bat turned into a load of bat-shit crazy. This was one of those times, Coco decided. "Mrs. Carter, what have I told you about letting strangers into the house?"

"Did I get everything right, Alex?" Mrs. Carter asked.

"Every detail, Mrs. C." Alex patted her hand. "Every detail."

"If I were thirty years younger, I'd take up with that man. The things I could teach him." Mrs. Carter set off on a rant.

When she was done, Alex said, "Carlos' loss, Mrs. C. Carlos' loss."

The smile twisted Mrs. Carter's lips. "You are as sweet as you are smart."

"I only speak the truth, Mrs. C," Alex said with a wink.

Coco only lifted a brow. The whole scene felt as if she'd been sucked into an episode of the Twilight Zone.

"Back to what I was saying. I've discussed this with Alex, and I believe it's in your best interest to accept the offer, dear." Mrs. Carter sipped coffee; her pinky daintily flipped high.

"What offer? What are you talking about, Mrs. Carter?"

"I've given him my permission to whisk you off on that plane of his. So, go on, finish your coffee and get to packing your bags."

Eyes wide lifted to Mrs. Carter. "You're serious. He's a P.A. whatever that is."

"A personal assistant," Alex put in.

"Sure. Okay. And you work for Carlo D'Onofrio, and you're here to pick me up." The sarcasm in Coco's voice rang clear.

"He is. Why would he make that up, dear?" Mrs. Carter topped Alex's coffee.

Coco's face held just enough shock now. "He's really here to take me to the airport to see Carlo?"

"That's what I said, dear, and I'm going with you. I'll be serving as your chaperone."

"You are?"

"She is. I've cleared it with Mr. D'Onofrio. You're going to love it there, Mrs. C." Alex unbuttoned his jacket and sank to the depths of the couch, his arm stretching across the back.

"I know I am. Now, Alex, you help yourself to more biscuits while Coco and I pack."

"You take your time. I can eat your cookies all day long, Mrs. C."

"Well, don't just sit there with your mouth open, dear. Get upstairs and get packing," Mrs. Carter commanded, signalling Coco off the couch.

Chapter 12

STANDING ON THE terrace sipping Kristal, Coco took a scan of the view. Miles of glinting white beach hemmed the blue Pacific Ocean that stretched far and wide to meet a cloudless sky. Oiled bodies spread out on colourful towels strewn over the sand, soaked sun. The scent of cocoa butter mingled with salt and brine riding on the mist from the sea.

Coco heard the steady drone of waves as they rolled in and pulled back out. Children's laughter mingled with the exchange of lingo unique to the surfers who crowded the beach.

Coco thought she could get used to this.

Leaning on the terrace's glass railing, Coco aimed her eyes toward Carlo's house, a modern architectural structure of concrete and glass. Potted blooms along the border of the terrace spilled from rectangle planters. The large unblinded glass wall offered a view of the sparkling white kitchen, the dining room, and Carlo's bedroom on the level above.

Coco wondered how many women he'd entertained in that room and if it was the reason she was there. She'd read about the revolving door of women that traipsed in and out of Carlo's life. There had been leading ladies and models that graced runways and magazine covers, a princess or two. She was none of those things. So what was she doing there?

Her curiosity would soon be put to rest when Carlo, trailed by the brown-haired Chihuahua, joined her on the terrace.

He wore jeans and a buttoned-down white shirt with the sleeves rolled to the elbows. The sleeves of the canary-yellow sweater around his shoulders were knotted at his chest. He wore tan loafers on sockless feet and looked every bit the Californian.

"You like the view?" He sank his tall frame into the soft cushion of the lounge chair while the big-eared dog with the large, brown eyes curled at his feet.

"It's breathtaking." Coco sat in the chair next to him when he signalled her to join him. "Thank you for the invitation, the private plane ride, the Kristal, and the opportunity to enjoy this." She gestured widely. "Who's your friend?"

"This is Fredo." The dog raised one eye than the other before slipping back to sleep. "He's a rescue who's been with me for a few months." Carlo reached for the bottle sitting on ice and poured himself a flute of Kristal. Taking a long sip of his drink, he studied Coco's face. There was light in the Jade green eyes and a smile on her lips. "This suits you."

"Can't argue with you there." Coco waved at the woman on the beach. She wore checked knee-high shorts, a floral blouse, and a floppy-brimmed hat over her peppered hair. Walking alongside her, Alex pointed out the points of interest. "That's Mrs. Carter. She and Alex hit it off from the moment they met."

"He misses my mom, whom he considered his adoptive mother," Carlo said. "I first met Alex on the set of Rumpelstiltskin, an off-off-Broadway show I sponsored. He was a young wannabe actor working as a stagehand. He approached me and asked me to read a God-awful play he'd written. I sat down with him and...."

"Told him it was okay and that he had potential."

Carlo smiled. "No. I told him the truth. That it was the worst dribble I'd read and that he'd never make it as a writer."

"Hmmm. You are lucky you're good looking because subtlety is also not one of your strong suits either."

Bemused eyebrows raised. "He was in his late teens. I'd seen him pocketing food from the buffet table backstage."

"So you took it from him or accused him of...."

Carlo cut Coco off midstream. "Christ woman, do you ever shut up?" Smirking, Coco bit her bottom lip. "Better. I found out he was living on the streets for a couple of years, had been since ageing out of the system. He was an orphan fostered for years. I invited him to dinner and offered him a job as my P.A. I'd seen him work and determined him to be organized, creative, and enthusiastic." Carlo refilled his glass and Coco's when she held her glass out.

"But before he could become my P.A., I made him promise me to finish high school. He agreed. He enrolled, and while he attended school, I had him move into my old room at my mom's house. My father had passed on, and my brothers and sisters were off to school and starting their new lives. My mother was thrilled for the company. She and Alex became close. She treated him as her son." Carlo reached down to pet Fredo when he stirred at his feet.

Coco's heart swelling, she stared at Carlo over the rim of her flute. The man was the antithesis of everything she was. Why would he align himself with her?

"Anyway, Alex not only completed high school, but he got himself a Master's degree in management. He's been with me ever since and is the best damn P.A. I've had and a great friend. He keeps me organized, and his research is impeccable. He reads every script sent to me. His instincts for choosing the right ones have been dead on. Everyone thinks I scout the talent back home, but it's actually Alex. He makes his recommendations, and I look them over, but Alex has been spot on every single time. Alex is family."

"He can't pass as your family."

"Why, because he's black?"

"No, it's because, from the sounds of it, he's smarter than you."

Carlo let out a booming laugh. "You're not wrong there." Carlo reached in to brush the hair from her face when the wind carried it. "It was Alex who suggested I bring you out here. Do you like it here?"

Coco aimed quizzical eyes at him. "I can get used to this. I can sink my teeth into the whole Los Angeles scene."

"Would you consider moving to L.A. and in here with me?"

"Jesus. I...." she faltered, stared at him for another moment. "Are you serious?"

"Dead serious."

Coco debated how to play her next move. Should she play the honest card, the coy, or the needy card? He had her off her game, and she rose and walked to the edge of the terrace to put distance between them.

Understanding her need to think things through, he waited a few moments before walking to her.

He leaned against the rail, crossed his feet at the ankles. "What are you thinking, Coco? You can tell me anything." She remained quiet, so he added a little more warmth to his smile. "Tell me what's on your mind."

"You tell me what's on yours first? I have a feeling there's a lot more on yours than mine."

Carlo met her eyes with a firm stare. "I want you to marry me."

Swallowing the obstruction in her throat, she stared at him. "What? What are you…?" Words dried up.

"You heard, and you heard, right."

"You don't even know me. You left me hanging the day following your invitation to dinner. You chose Busty-Milligan over me. You…."

"I get the point. I'm sorry I left without notice. Something came up, and I had to fly back right that night. And as I recall, it was you who left me waiting out in the limo. I waited for you for half an hour before they told me you'd left through the back door." He took the lighter from her and, flicking it on, lit the cigarette she slipped between her lips. "Miss Mulligan was the right candidate to choose. She's very talented."

Coco studied him through the haze of exhaled smoke. Killer body and D-cups, no matter the century, translated to talent. Men were so unoriginal.

"Then, marry her." The ice in her voice could freeze the ocean before them.

Christ, he loved those green eyes when they blazed fire. She was a pistol loaded with fuck-you bullets, and she was perfect. He'd play her game with his own brand of logic.

"I never saw Miss Mulligan in that way, but now that you mention it, I can see the possibility. I'm sorry I brought it up and upset you." Carlo pushed off the railing and started to head into the house, and Fredo mimicked him.

Her little ploy failed miserably. Christ, everything was jumbled and tangled together. She had to stop reacting from gut emotion, Coco told herself. She was in over her head where Carlo was concerned.

Feeling the sensation of drowning take hold, Coco opted to say what was on her mind. "Why do you want to marry me? You don't know me."

Carlo's lips curled, but he put on a straight face when he turned to face her. "I know you better than you think. The fact you stood me up the night I invited you to dinner tells me you're a woman who lives life by her rules. The fact you crossed the homophobe line of demonstrators protesting outside the theatre where *I'm A Man* played for weeks tells me you're a tolerant and principled woman. The fact you punched one of those protesters when they verbally attacked Jazzie for being who he is, as God made him, as he made his way into the theatre, tells me that under that tough exterior is the heart of a caring woman."

The slash of dark eyebrows rose. "How do you know all this? Did you have me followed?"

"I own the theatre. I got the police report and invoice when the man you punched demanded his hospital bill for the broken nose you caused to be paid by the theatre."

"Shit, sorry. I didn't know. Still, he's lucky that's all I broke." Coco set her glass on the railing with a snap when she remembered the vile words the ignorant pig lobbed at Jazzie made her see red.

God! He loved this girl. "Not that I condone violence, but it tells me you take no prisoners when someone's in need."

"You have to stand up for what's right. Otherwise, what's the point of your existence on this earth?"

"And that right there is why I admire you."

"You admire me."

Nodding, Carlo reached for her hand, squeezed it. "Very much, and it's why I believe we're a good fit."

"Why do you want to get married? As I see it, you have a perfect life. Why weigh it down with marriage."

"Have you ever heard the saying, all that glitters is not gold? I'm thirty-seven, and, according to my mother, I need a wife to make me look respectable. And you don't defy my mother."

"I'm only nineteen."

"Going on forty, and it's not like that at all. As I see it, you need a guardian angel. We can help each other, Coco. You want your face on the big screen. I can make your dream a reality." Carlo watched Coco aim eyes at the terns that landed along the water's edge, their heads bobbing as they searched for food. "I told you, you have potential. I'll have the best acting coach in Hollywood work with you. In a year, you'll be ready, and I'll have you cast as my leading lady in a script I've been sitting on. The leading part in *The Mistress of Covington* was written for you."

"You can do that?"

"You'd be surprised what a male headliner can do in this business. As long as I keep the theatres filled and generating revenue, they'll accommodate me at every turn. Besides, once you've had the training you need, getting you cast won't be a hard sell."

The happiness swelling inside her threatened to erupt into laughter and tears like a long-dormant volcano. She was this much closer to seeing her name in lights. And Christ, to have her name headlining alongside Carlo D'Onofrio's was beyond her wildest dreams.

That she had to promise him marriage when she knew nothing about him was a minuscule price to pay, and she said, "Yes, I'll marry you, Carlo, but we'll need to set some ground rules."

With a quick laugh, he said, "A Hollywood marriage wouldn't survive otherwise."

Once again, Alex was right. She was perfect.

Chapter 13

THE MORE COCO learned of Carlo's reasons for wanting to marry her, the more she knew she'd made the right decision to accept his proposal.

The ground rules set and agreed to by the soon-to-be bride and groom, Coco, set off to start the next chapter of her life. The world was finally on her side and steering the life she deserved her way.

Mrs. Carter and Coco began to plan the spare-no-expense fall wedding. The Carolina Herrera silk strapless A-line wedding dress with an embroidered corset that flattered Coco's curves was selected from the many designs submitted by prominent designers. The prestigious Bel-Air Club booked years in advance, swiftly found an opening when Alex informed them it was for Carlo D'Onofrio's wedding.

The church was booked, and massive arrangements of hydrangeas, peonies, and gardenias were ordered and scheduled to fly in the day before the wedding. Julia Child, a good friend of Carlo's, was happy to plan the menu for the nine hundred celebrities, dignitaries, and who's-who of the corporate world. Coco and Mrs. Carter concurred with Julia's suggestion for a ten-tier vanilla sponge with espresso-infused buttercream cake.

Alex surprised Coco and Mrs. Carter when he told them Dean and Frank would be performing at the reception. It was their wedding gift to Carlo, their long-time friend. Mrs. Carter almost fainted at the news. That she would get to see two of her favourite performers in person and at her little girl's wedding was a dream come true.

Carlo surprised Coco by flying Aunt Abby to L.A. weeks before the wedding. On seeing the private jet and Coco's new home, Aunt Abby couldn't have been more thrilled at her niece's good fortune. Aunt Abby couldn't have been prouder of her protégé when Coco told her the terms she demanded before entering into wedded bliss.

"Darling, no marriage is ever the perfect bliss we imagine it to be. In every marriage, the pile of sweet honey eventually dissolves to unearth a mound of crap," Aunt Abby said with a sober nod.

"I'M GETTING MARRIED." COCO EYED THE glinting three-karat diamond on her finger with a wide smile.

"Married? You're nineteen years old." Mary's familiar disapproving tone flowed from the end of the telephone line while Emma quietly listened on the kitchen extension wide-eyed. "Who are you marrying? Does your aunt know?"

"Are you ready for this?" Coco said.

"Waiting with baited breath," Mary said.

Coco envisaged Mary's eye roll. "I'm marrying Carlo D'Onofrio."

Silence.

"You know who that is?" Coco waited a moment. "He's a big time actor. *Timeline, God's Child,* and *Surrender,* are some of his movies. Surely you've heard of them."

Silence.

"I have, Coco. They were excellent movies," Emma said when the silence persisted.

"Isn't he like ancient?" That from Mary.

"He is older, and yes, my aunt knows and approves. She's here helping me plan the wedding along with your aunt." Coco's lips curved when she pictured Mary's eyes popping out of their socket.

"Put my aunt on the phone. I need to speak with her," Mary demanded.

"Mary, your auntie is having the time of her life. Carlo has a beachfront house in Malibu. Mrs. Carter spends her days with Aunt Abby, walking on the beach or sitting on the terrace soaking in the sun and sipping mimosas. Most days, she's sloshed by dinnertime," Coco added and stifled a laugh.

Mary fell back into the living room couch. "Christ, I knew you'd be a bad influence on my aunt. The woman is a saint who's led a sheltered life. She shouldn't be introduced to your life of debauchery."

"Oh, chill out, Mary. I'm joking. She's not sloshed most nights … only some." Coco bit back a snorting laugh.

Coco was egging Mary on and getting under her skin. Mary felt immediately more irritated with herself for allowing it. With a flash of temper, Mary snapped, "You're such a bitch, Coco."

Coco chuckled. "I'm all that, but you're too easy, Mary. What do you say, Emma? You're always quiet, but I know you have an opinion. Do you think I'm making a mistake?"

"What I think is not important. You're going to do what you've set your mind on doing. It's how you're built, Coco. If this is what you want, I'll support you, Coco," Emma said.

Emma knew her well, Coco thought. "Thank you, Emma. I can always count on you."

Mary followed the comment with an "Mmm-hmm" as she imagined the relief swarming Emma.

By Emma's reasoning, with Coco married, the chance of Steve getting back with her disintegrated, and he'd move on. Steve would forget Coco, and Emma now stood a chance with Steve. Mary knew better. Steve was too in love with Coco to forget her.

"I'm happy for you, Coco, and I hope you are too. Carlo's a good looking man, and he doesn't seem to be anything like the self-centred, need-constant-stroking celebrities we're accustomed to." Emma's mind swirled with thoughts of how Steve would take the news. He was going to be devastated.

"Thank you, Emma." Coco could always count on Emma to be a loyal friend. "Mary, are you there?"

"I'm here," Mary replied coolly.

"Be happy for me, Mary. Carlo is what I need. He's spoiling me rotten and promised to put me in one of his movies to set my career in motion."

And there it was, quid pro quo, Mary thought. The marriage wasn't based on love. Genuine male-female relationships weren't for Coco. Mary wondered what she'd promised Carlo in exchange for getting what she wanted.

"He's old, Coco, but aside from the fact, he's old enough to be your father, he's a man of the world. Have you really thought this through?"

Mary, the mother of reason, Coco thought. "Christ, Mary, for once stop being so guarded. So ... so ...."

"Prudent, logical, rational," Mary finished. "I have more adjectives."

"Jesus, Mary, you can be such a downer. Maybe if you got laid, you wouldn't be such a bitch." The tempered response was classic Coco deflecting from the real issue.

"Sleeping with every guy I meet isn't high on my list. I'm focused on my studies."

"Maybe, it should be."

"I'll see if I can dig me up a geriatric to spread my legs for."

Coco pinched the bridge of her nose between her thumb and forefinger. Leave it to Mary to aggravate her at her good fortune. "I have thought this through. It's what I want, what I need to do. What happened to 'we're a team? We support one another no matter what.' Emma, what do you say?" Coco added, knowing she could always coax Emma into her corner.

Emma pressed lips together. As much as she agreed with Mary's reasoning, she didn't dare come between Mary and Coco when the punches flew between them. Besides, she had more pressing issues than Coco's selfishness on her mind. Emma's thoughts were on Steve and how he was going to be affected by the news.

Almost one year later and the man was still pining for her. The news of Coco's marriage was going to devastate him. After everything Steve had done for Coco, the things he'd put up with. Sometimes Coco could be a selfish bitch. He deserved better.

"It's your life, Coco. You know I'm all about live and let live. I just wished you cared more about how this is going to affect ... some people."

Coco rolled her eyes skyward. "If by some people, you mean Steve he needs to move on. I have. Jesus, it's been months since I left and completely cut contact."

Shelving her irritation, Emma kept her voice light. "Coco, he's still asking me where you are, how he can get in touch with you. I'm running out of excuses."

"By the end of the week, you won't have to cover for me anymore. The press release is going out. The news will be all over the news." The irritation edged into Coco's voice was a by-product of her guilt.

Coco knew the news would kill Steve, but she had to do what was best for her. Nothing Emma or Mary could say would change her mind. Carlo was going to be instrumental in helping forge her path onto the big screen, and one day, she'd be bigger than both of them could imagine.

"Why you bother, Emma, I don't know. Everyone always has to clean up after her. It's always all about her," Mary said.

"If the only thing I can get from my two best friends for my wedding announcement is judgement, rebuking, and resentment to my good fortune…."

"If you think we envy you, think again, Coco." Mary laughed bitterly.

"You can both go to hell. Consider yourselves uninvited. In three months, I'm getting married, and I don't want either of you at my wedding." Coco hung up before Emma or Mary could get a word in.

"Oh, Mary, we're horrible friends." Regret stirred inside Emma when she joined Mary in the living room. "I didn't want it to end up like this."

"I know." Mary glanced out the window, where the rain came down in a thick wall of water.

"We should call her and apologize."

Slumped on the couch, her head resting against its back, Mary said, "You know when she gets in a mood, she won't take our calls. Let her cool down. When she does, she'll realize we're only thinking about her well-being, and she'll call us back." I hope.

Chapter 14

Fall 2002

FROM HER BEDROOM window, Emma watched an angry Mary circle the grounds and wondered what Coco had done to cause Mary to be so angry.

Mary and Coco's friendship had always been contentious, but like magnets, opposites attract. Mary was too inflexible, too pragmatic and Coco was on the far opposite of that spectrum. When push came to shove, they were friends first, and they always made up.

Emma hoped it was the case now as she watched Mary agitatedly pace while conducting a conversation with herself. Brow arched, Emma curiously observed Mary's hand going to fists before raising them in the air as if in prayer. Then gripping the paddock's fence, she dropped her head in defeat. Mary remained that way for some time before she straightened, and sucking a breath, reached for the sunglasses nestled in her hair. Sliding them on, she followed the path back to the resort.

Emma hoped that meant Mary had cooled off.

The anger poured hot out of Mary when she stormed out of the living room and left Emma and Coco staring after her. Emma had no clue why Mary reacted so angrily, but she supposed Coco knew the reason. Emma wouldn't ask, not yet. Coco was so rattled by Mary's reaction that Emma thought it best not to bring it up.

Emma wasn't ready to deal with their drama, which she suspected went beyond slight and words between friends. The anger and resentment in Mary's eyes for Coco was almost certainly the reason for Coco's sudden disappearance from their lives a decade ago after reappearing out of nowhere.

For now, Emma decided to make the best of her weekend spa. Unlike Coco and Mary, Emma wouldn't get another chance to indulge in such luxury, and she had a complimentary facial to get to in ten minutes she wasn't about to miss.

FEELING REVITALIZED AND PAMPERED AFTER THE hour-long facial, Emma decided to stay in the moment by indulging in a sweet treat. A cup of coffee and a piece of cheesecake or possibly one of those butter tarts she'd seen wheeled on the dessert cart would do the trick.

Her mouth-watering at the thought, Emma followed the stone path from the spa to the lodge. Above her, a pair of blue jays winged by in a sun-drenched, blue sky. She watched two women mount horses with the help of the stable hand and mulled, signing up for the riding lessons that came with her stay. When would she get the opportunity to indulge in horseback riding if she didn't do it now?

Right now, she had cheesecake on her mind. Nearing the lodge, the familiar voices flowing from the garden at the side of the house caught Emma's attention. She stopped to listen.

"What are you doing, Coco? Why are you here?" Mary folded her arms across her chest.

"I live here."

"Since when? Our agreement was you'd go back to Los Angeles, far away from Emma."

"I wanted to see both of you."

"We had an agreement, Coco. You were going to disappear and leave Emma alone to live her life. It shouldn't have been difficult for you to do. Disappearing is what you do best." Mary's eyes fired daggers.

"I know, I agreed, but I need to talk to you and Emma."

"Christ, you've never cared about anyone but yourself, Coco. The world doesn't revolve around you, and we're no longer kids who'll put up with your shit. I want you to leave Emma and me alone." Lava-hot Anger poured out of Mary.

"Please, Mary, I don't mean to intrude in your lives. I just want to talk to my friends."

"Pfft, friends, you don't know the meaning."

"Please, Mary, I know you're angry, and you have every right to be. I don't expect forgiveness, but…."

"You're expecting forgiveness after what you did. How you even have the nerve to show your face is beyond me? But then you've always been a selfish bitch."

Coco pushed past the hurtful jab. "Just a conversation, Mary, and I'll be out of your life afterward. I promise."

Emma rounded the house and startled both women. "I don't want you to disappear from our lives, my life again, Coco?" To Mary, she said, "I don't want you to disappear either. I miss you both. I want you to stop fighting and demand you tell me what's going on between you because it has to do with me from what I just overheard. What is it you're not telling me?" Emma asked and watched their guilty eyes cut away from her.

Chapter 15

THE DAY FOLLOWING her conversation with Coco determined to ease the blow for Steve, Emma showed up at his house. Before he heard it in the news, telling him of Coco's engagement in person was the right thing to do. Steve deserved that much.

Emma cut across the grass in the front yard. She walked up the narrow stone path parallel to the brown-brick house, past the bushes, with flowering red roses to the gate. Throwing the latch on the gate, Emma walked toward the basement entrance. A screen door shielded the wood door. It took her a while to embrace the idea of knocking on the door. She turned to walk away. It was then she heard the door open.

"Emma, hi," he said, pushing the screen door open. In his hand, he had a black garbage bag.

His tousled hair was sprinkled with wood shavings, the bare chest smooth and hard as steel, and his flushed face sheened with sweat. His jeans hung low on his hips. Sweet and sour Jesus, he was gorgeous, she thought, feeling a fierce pull at her belly.

Emma stared at him without speaking for a long while. Then with a shaky breath, she said, "Hi."

"I was about to toss this out. What brings you here?" Steve wiped his face with the T-shirt draped on his shoulder.

"I'm sorry to bother you. Do you have a minute?"

"Sure, let me toss this out." She stepped aside to let him by. "Go on in. I'll be right back."

Emma walked in. The basement apartment was long and narrow and, to her surprise, stylish. The floor was dark wood, and the walls were steel blue. There was a tan leather couch with a matching chair. A steamer trunk served as the coffee table and storage. Across from the sofa, a low table had a portable TV set. Along the right wall, a galley-style kitchen was a work in progress.

Straight ahead, on the facing wall, a platform bed was covered with a white spread. The bed and the night tables with brass lamps and a clock radio sat on a thick, shag carpet. Sport-related framed prints hung on the walls.

Cupboard doors recently installed and varnished sat open to dry. A long, speckled granite top rested against the wall. A Sparkling new, white refrigerator, stove, and microwave fit snuggly amongst the cabinetry.

The room was innately masculine and reflected his taste and style.

Steve was back in a couple of minutes. "This is my humble home." Steve helped her out of her trench coat. In the peach blouse tucked into slim-fitting jeans, she looked casually stylish.

"It's a nice place." The cloud of honey-brown hair rained around the pretty face with rosy pink cheeks when she shed her beanie hat and handed it to him.

"Thanks. I'm a mess. Can you and give me a minute to take a quick shower?"

That sent her imagination racing. "Sure. Yeah. I can wait."

"Make yourself at home." Steve gestured for her to take a seat on the couch. "Sorry for the mess. It's a work in progress." He disappeared through a door to her right and left it slightly ajar. "I've been working on the kitchen cupboards all morning," he said, loud enough for his voice to be heard over the sound of running water.

"It's looking good," she said, with images of water running over his naked body crowding her mind. He tormented her for ten minutes.

When he walked out of the bathroom, he wore jeans and dragged a black T-shirt over the broad shoulders. He smelled of Irish Spring. He'd raked his fingers through his wet hair, and Emma could see the tips curling with dampness.

Emma took a steadying breath and gripped the purse on her lap tighter as she watched him, admiring the fit of his jeans when he crossed to the refrigerator.

"Would you like one?" Steve waved the beer bottle in the air.

Unable to speak, she shook her head.

Taking a pull of his beer, he studied Emma. "Are you all right, Emma?" She always looked antsy at their encounters—he didn't dare refer to them as dates—but today, more so than usual.

Unable to get information of Coco's whereabouts on their second date, Steve asked Emma out on a third and fourth date. With each passing date, he came to enjoy their time together more than he imagined he would.

Coco's hold on him, however, wouldn't allow Steve to move on with his life. To wash the guilt of betrayal away, Steve spontaneously bumped into Emma at the end of her shifts. At Java Joe, across from the supermarket, they grabbed a coffee. A few minutes in, Steve forgot why he was there and fell easily into conversation, and Emma listened. Unlike Coco, Emma didn't judge or scorn Steve's plans, dreams, and choices as Coco always did.

That cup of coffee led to twice-weekly "impromptu coffee encounters" that Steve and Emma looked forward to.

"Is everything all right, Emma?" The weary look in her eyes had him setting his beer bottle aside. Pinching her chin, he tilted her face up, so their eyes met. "What is it, Emma?"

"Coco," she started to say and immediately saw the change in his eyes. Regret swamped her.

"What about Coco? Emma, tell me already," he urged.

"She's engaged, getting married in a few months." Her heart dropped at the expression of loss that filled his eyes. Her heart wept for him and her.

Face pale, eyes dazed, Steve murmured, "Engaged? Married? What are you talking about?"

"She, um, called last night to tell Mary and me. I'm sorry, Steve."

The injured expression was evident on his face. Steve closed his eyes as the pain stabbed at him.

"She's getting married in a few months, in Los Angeles." Emma held back the who, feeling it would add insult to injury. Pride in an injured man was fragile. "I thought it best you hear it from me instead of reading about it in the papers. I'm sorry, Steve. I'm so sorry."

The hurt was so sharp it knocked the wind out of him. He gasped for air.

"Breath, Steve, breath."

"Who? What do you mean by seeing it in the papers? Who's she marrying?" The oncoming headache was expanding inside his skull, and he massaged fingers at his temple.

"It doesn't matter who. Can I get you an Aspirin?"

"No, but I'll take a shot of whiskey. Bottle and glass are in the pantry next to the refrigerator." He angled his head. "Who, Emma, who's she marrying?" He watched Emma silently pour two fingers into a glass and walk the bottle and glass to Steve. "Who, Emma? Tell me."

"Carlo D'Onofrio."

"The movie star?" Steve said when he connected the name to The Rival, one of his favourite movies.

She nodded. "I'm sorry, Steve."

His eyes went grim. "Coco certainly traded up. I never stood a chance." In one gulp, Steve sent the whiskey streaming down his throat. The burn felt good.

"She's not marrying for love, Steve. He's promised to get her into the movies."

"That's a consolation, isn't it?" Steve took another gulp of whiskey straight from the bottle. "You've known all along."

"No, I didn't," Emma said in earnest. She always believed Coco would be back once she realized she couldn't make it in the big league.

"But you knew where she was all this time. All those times I asked you, you knew. You should have told me, Emma. I could have gone after her changed her mind. Why didn't you tell me?" The eyes that cut into her showed pain, hurt, and misplaced love.

Guilt balling in her, Emma aimed her eyes downward. "She asked me not to say where she was."

"I could have prevented this if I'd contacted her."

The look Emma sent him was sombre and apologetic. "No, Steve, you couldn't have. Coco's mind was set long ago, before she met you, to go off in search of this acting dream of hers. I'm sorry, but it's the truth, Steve." The words made his eyes go so sharp she thought they would strike her down if he had the power to do so, but she plowed on. "I know it hurts. I also know you know I'm right."

Steve lowered his gaze.

"I'm sorry, Steve."

"Stop saying that," he snarled. Snatching the bottle, he poured, took the drink in one swallow. The whiskey burned straight down to the sickness in his belly. "I want you to go. Go." Heat flashed in the dark eyes.

Emma didn't budge. His feelings of violation, fear, and anger were a classic reaction to the grief consuming him. She cursed Coco. How could she not care about the hurt and heartache she caused him?

She wasn't Coco, and she cared.

Taking a deep forbearing breath, Emma said, "I'm not leaving you alone. You need a friend right now. We can talk. We can order a pizza, watch a movie, or just sit here quietly. Whatever you want. I'm staying put." Her tone was firm, but the blue eyes that met Steve when he lifted his head were tender, caring and loving, and the smile she flashed him was warm.

She always smoothed the pain away and made him feel whole. Gratitude flooded him, and he leaned in to brush his lips over hers tenderly. Before she could catch her breath, Steve covered her mouth with his. The kiss was violent and greedy, but there was a kind of precise flourish in the way he took her mouth.

Emma heard her heart drumming in her ears, felt her stomach do somersaults. It was her first kiss, and it was glorious. It was as remarkable as she imagined it would be. And it was with Steve.

His tongue found hers, tangled and danced. The soft moan she let out couldn't be mistaken for anything other than need and want.

Reacting on impulse, Steve scooped her off the couch and carried her to the bed. Laying her down, he brushed back the hair that curtained her face. Eye to eye, Emma looked into the dark eyes as familiar to her as her own. In them, she saw the desire for her she never imagined she would. He wanted her. Her heart swelled.

She'd dreamt of this moment for so long, and now that it was here, she wasn't sure she was ready. She wasn't as experienced as Coco. She was a virgin and in way over her head.

Emma felt her lungs choke up when she felt his fingers tug at her shirt buttons and his hands skimmed over her skin to the snap on her jeans. Her breath hitched when he slid her jeans and cotton panties over her hips.

She winced at the thought she wore purple polka dot, cotton briefs today, but she never imagined she'd end up here.

Her eyes fixed wide when he moved to shed his T-shirt. His shoulders and arms were tanned and muscular, his chest solid. God, she wanted to touch him just to assure herself this wasn't a dream. But thoughts, so many rolled in her mind.

What would Coco say to her sleeping with Steve?

How would Coco react?

Would Coco give her blessings if she knew how Coco felt about Steve?

Would Coco even care?

Whether Coco did or not, guilt washed over Emma. This wasn't what a friend did to another.

When he shed his jeans, the doubtful lines that creased Emma's face vanished. He was fully aroused and bigger than life. She did that.

She'd seen photographs of naked men, but nothing prepared her for how impressive he was. His waist tapered to narrow hips where dark hair was stark against pearl-white skin. His legs were long, muscular.

The unabashed arousal set Emma's cheeks ablaze. Her loins burned, and her eyes swam with lust. She trembled out of fear and anticipation.

The smile of satisfaction on Steve's face was one of pure delight, and before she knew it, he was on top of her pinning her down with his hard body. His skin felt hot. He smelled sweet.

He filled her veins with fire. Every nerve ending exploded in unison. Shock, awareness, and want flickered into her eyes.

There was no going back now.

Mouth to mouth, she felt the heat of his breath on her face. The scent of man, his fully aroused body pressing down, awakened the dormant woman in her. She couldn't fight the feeling of want that had been inside her forever detonating. Gripped by the dreamlike moment full of promise, Emma felt her self-control slipping from her grasp. Emma's need to be with him grew strong.

Glands could overpower friendship and loyalty, Emma thought, as she yielded to him.

Chapter 16

ONE MONTH AFTER their telephone conversation, Coco hadn't called, and pride barred Mary from picking up the telephone, as did the guilt in Emma for sleeping with Steve.

It shamed Emma as much to know as to admit she'd slept with Steve and the secret of her most glorious night remained concealed in her head. But it was etched in her brain, and Emma couldn't stop thinking of Steve or their night together.

Steve touched her in all the right places, in all the right ways to set her blood humming and nerves singing. As much as she wanted a repeat performance, Emma hadn't been able to face him since that night. The feeling of betrayal marred the best night of her life shared with the man she deeply loved.

Now that she discovered she was pregnant with Steve's child, the most notable event of her life had turned into her worst decision.

As much as Emma wanted Steve's baby, the guilt made it impossible to relish in the moment. Whether because her hormones were playing havoc on her emotions or because the panic of the impossible situation she got herself into rode on her nerves, Emma's mind raced. Questions and doubts crowded her mind.

Steve's and her young age was the least of Emma's worries.

Steve initiated their sexual encounter, but he'd conclude she'd planned to get pregnant and force him into marriage. As much as men equally contributed to an unplanned pregnancy, women were blamed and held to account.

Emma didn't want to tie Steve into something he didn't want. What was she to do? Her situation wasn't the kind of thing you could box away.

Everything was so screwed up.

At nineteen, Emma was pregnant by her best friend's ex-lover's baby. While Coco didn't care about Steve, she had a hold on him that made him unable to let go of her, and Emma would never exist in his eyes.

Sometimes life becomes a poorly directed movie, and as always, Emma was the leading lady.

Emma knew Steve slept with her to smooth his pain, but she let it happen because Emma hoped he'd see *her*. Steve hadn't. She'd been a physical outlet for his anger. Steve used her as a means to ease his broken heart and strike back at Coco.

How could she tell him she was pregnant?

Emma eyed her profile in the mirror. She never imagined she'd end up pregnant the one time she had sex. But she was, and now she was in a predicament.

Emma would never do the unthinkable, not because her religion didn't permit it, but because it wasn't the moral thing to do. She'd made the mistake, and she'd own it. Besides, since she could remember being a wife and mother was what she'd ever wanted.

She was a simple girl with simple dreams.

Looking at herself in the mirror, Emma stroked her belly. She was carrying a life in her—Steve's and hers.

"What are you doing?" Mary's voice had Emma swirling to face the opening bedroom door.

A guilty smile flirted around Emma's eyes. "How long have you been standing there?"

Mary walked into the room Emma shared with her sister Maddie. It hadn't changed since Emma was a kid. Pink walls were covered in posters of John Travolta in his iconic white suit, Madonna and Whitney Houston. On Maddie's side of the room, the posters were more youthful: Big Bird, Donny Osmond, and David Cassidy.

The room was neat and orderly, as it always was. The dresser, two single beds, and the night table between them were as old as Emma was and polished to a shine. That was due to Emma's obsession for neatness, not Maddie's.

Mary, Coco, and Emma had spent countless nights in that room doing what girls do. They talked about boys while applying makeup and eating the great pizza Emma's mom always made for them. With the window cracked open, they tried smoking their first cigarette after Emma snuck one from her father's pack. Emma and Mary got sick to their stomach and never took up the habit while Coco handled it like a pro.

"Long enough." Mary tossed her coat on Emma's bed. "You need to stop obsessing about your weight."

"I wasn't."

"It's me, Emma. You can admit it to me." Mary fell back onto the edge of the bed.

"Honestly, I wasn't," Emma repeated.

"Mmm-hmm. So, what did you want to talk to me about? What was so important we couldn't do it over the phone?" Mary watched Emma walk to her and sit next.

"You still haven't heard from Coco?"

Emma gnawing on her bottom lip was pure Emma, Mary thought. "You could have asked me that over the phone?" Mary settled back on her elbows, set her eyes up to the popcorn ceiling. "No, I haven't heard from Coco, and no, I'm not calling her. Why are you feeling so guilty, Emma? She's the one who hung up on us. She should be the one calling."

Emma inclined her head. "How could you not feel guilty? We're not going to be at her wedding."

"Don't worry. It won't be her only one." As serious as Mary was, Emma felt the smile break through. "I'm not joking. I peg Coco for a minimum of three marriages. So, you have nothing to feel guilty about."

Emma heaved a sigh. "I do. That's why I wanted to speak to you." Emma pushed to her feet, walked to the dresser and picked up a brush to run through her hair. "You're the strong one amongst us who always speaks her mind. I need your opinion."

The seriousness in Emma's voice made Mary sit up. "What about?"

Emma pressed her lips together as she ran the brush through her hair and gathered her nerves. Mary wasn't going to be kind or polite. She wasn't going to mince her words, and she was going to preach. Not the reaction Emma wanted, but she needed to tell someone about her pregnancy. She needed guidance and help to sort out her muddled thoughts.

Emma needed Mary's sharp mind to help steer her in the right direction.

"What is it, Emma? What's wrong?"

Emma needed to tell Mary. Swallowing her pride in one gulp, Emma blurted, "I slept with Steve." She'd expected an outburst from Mary, but an unnerving silence was all she got. When the silence lingered, Emma said, "Say something, Mary."

"Jesus, Emma, what do you want me to say when you drop a bomb like that?" Mary's eyes followed Emma as she walked to the bedroom door. "Not that I'm surprised. I mean, I know how you've felt for him all these years, but…."

"It's the, but that has my stomach churning. How am I to tell Coco?" Emma flipped the lock on the closed door to keep her nosy siblings out of the room.

"That's not what I was going to say."

At Mary's hesitation, Emma nudged her. "Just say what's on your mind. You always do. Don't stop now."

"Okay, it's not as if I'm going to say anything you don't already know. You just need to hear it said aloud. Steve's in love with Coco. He can't see beyond her. His heart will never be yours, Emma. Getting involved with Steve will only result in heartbreak. Don't you want someone who loves you back, Emma?"

Everything Mary said, Emma knew. It still didn't stop the pain from washing over her in turbulent waves, and she fell silent.

"I'm sorry, Emma. You asked."

"I did, and as you said, I know all this and needed to hear it out loud. The problem is that there's more at stake than my heart now."

"What are you saying?" In the ensuing silence, the pieces came together in Mary's head. Emma stroking her belly in front of the mirror and the urgency to speak to her in person. Mary's head jerked up. "Oh. Jesus, Emma, you're not." Emma's silence confirmed Mary's suspicion.

"Christ, Emma, you're pregnant with Steve's baby. How far along are you?"

"One month."

Mary shoved off the bed to stalk the room. "Why would you put yourself in such a precarious position?"

"It just happened."

"Nothing just happens, Emma. It takes actions, which you could have stopped at any point." Mary heard Emma's mother barking orders for everyone to get to the dinner table float through the closed bedroom door. "Jesus, does your mother know?"

"No one knows. I only found out a couple of days ago. I think she'll understand. She had me at the same age."

"Do I need to point out the obvious?"

Emma cracked the door open a few inches and yelled, "We'll be down in a minute, Mom." Closing the door again, she turned to Mary. "What's obvious?"

"Your mother was married when she had you? She's not going to understand her nineteen-year-old single daughter who doesn't even have a boyfriend being pregnant."

Coco was right. Mary was a downer, Emma thought, plunking down on the bed.

"I know, minor detail, but there it is. Have you told Steve?"

"That's what I wanted you to help me decide. Do you think I should?" Blue, mystified eyes gazed at Mary.

Sometimes Emma's innocence was that of a child's, Mary thought. But Emma wasn't a child. She was a woman with a life growing inside her.

Mary spoke gently now. "Steve's the father, Emma. He needs to know."

The innocence in Emma's eyes faded into unease. "But he's going to think I did this to entrap him."

"He can think what he wants. He had a hand in this and needs to take responsibility. You can't do this on your own, Emma. This is a baby we're talking about. This child will be dependent on you for everything, for the rest of its life."

Emma struggled not to let fear engulf her. "I know."

"And you need to tell Coco, not because you need her blessing. I mean, she's marrying some old geezer. She couldn't care less about Steve. You need to tell her because if I know you, the guilt of not telling her will consume you."

It was true enough, and Emma said, "I know."

"Now, you have a baby to keep healthy. Let's go get you some of your mother's delicious homemade pizza in you."

THAT NIGHT EMMA WROTE COCO A detailed letter. It contained the revelation of Steve and her. It outlined to Coco how badly Emma felt for her error in judgment. It had Emma's heartfelt apology and vow she'd never put a man above their friendship. It asked for Coco's forgiveness.

Emma read the letter over before she reached for the pen to sign it.

Chapter 17

SINCE HIS NIGHT with Emma, Steve had many women in his bed—a retaliatory response to the hurt and pain of losing Coco. There were blondes, brunettes, redheads, all one-night stands. None filled the hole in his heart. None was like Emma.

Emma listened to him, really listened. She laughed at his silly jokes. He and Emma had Coco in common. Emma knew Coco well and sympathized with him. Emma had been sympathetic enough to show up at his front door to tell him about Coco's engagement.

Steve missed Emma.

He needed someone to talk to. Steve needed someone to help him get through the hurt of Coco's very public engagement.

Coco was everywhere, on television, newspapers, and magazines. Everywhere he turned, he saw Coco flashing her quarter million-diamond ring, or kissing Carlo or looking deep into his eyes with a loving gaze. It drove Steve crazy, and the women he brought home wanted to hear none of his whining.

Steve needed someone to vent to. He needed Emma.

"Hi, Emma," Steve said when Emma stepped through the supermarket's sliding doors.

She looked tired. There were dark circles under her eyes, and her frizzed hair was tied back into a messy ponytail. Flyaway strands of hair hung over her face. She hadn't the energy to shed out of her work uniform and into her street clothes.

Emma stopped in her tracks and looked up. "Steve. What are you doing here?" It had been weeks since she last saw him, and didn't mask her surprise.

"Yeah, about not calling you, I'm sorry, I haven't…."

"You don't need to explain." She cut him off before he said something she'd regret.

"I was wondering if you'd like to join me for coffee." He gestured her to the side and away from the sliding doors to let exiting shoppers by.

"I'm exhausted, Steve. The cashier I hired to take the morning shift didn't show up, and I had to take it. I've been on my feet since six this morning."

It served her right for not taking the time to vet the new hire properly. But Emma had bigger things on her mind. She had a baby growing in her. A baby she couldn't afford, couldn't support, and certainly couldn't raise on her own. To top her troubles, she hadn't told her parents of the baby yet and lying to them was keeping her awake at night.

God, what she'd give to get a good night's sleep.

"Please, Emma. I need someone to talk to." Steve's voice cracked.

So do I, Steve, so do I. "I need to get home and off my feet." She spoke more sharply than he was used, and Steve took a moment to catch his breath.

Steve started to say something when the blond-haired, five-year-old girl darted through the sliding doors and bumped into him. She wore pink shorts, a white blouse with pink butterflies stamped throughout, and white sandals.

Steve crouched down, so they were eye to eye. "And where are you going, little lady?"

She aimed large blue eyes his way. "I'm not a little lady. I'm a little girl."

"And a very pretty one." Steve's comment got him a girlish giggle. "I'm Steve. What's your name?"

She stared back at Steve with a guarded look. "Mommy said not to speak to strangers."

"And she would be right. Where is your mommy?"

"She's inside talking to the lady who punches the machine."

"And you couldn't wait for her?"

She shook her head. Her blonde curls swayed with the movement. "She talks too much to the lady who punches the machine, and I want to get home to watch Big Bird."

"I can certainly understand that. Come on. I'll walk you to your car. Do you have your license and car keys?"

She snorted a laugh. "I don't drive, silly. I'm just a little girl. Mommy drives the station wagon."

"I see. Well, then, we better go find your mommy." Steve reached for the girl's hand. He was about to head inside the supermarket when the frantic woman came running through the doors. A profound sense of relief overcame her when she saw her daughter.

"There you are, Chrissie." She knelt and took the girl in a tight hug. "You gave me a fright when I couldn't find you." She pulled Chrissie in tighter.

"I'm sorry, Mommy. Steve was going to help me find you."

Chrissie's mother gave Steve a watery smile. "Thank you."

"No need for thanks." Steve twisted his lips into a smile. "Chrissie wanted to go home and watch Big Bird, but what she doesn't know is that Big Bird's a good friend of mine."

Chrissie's eyes went round. "He is."

Steve nodded. "And I know for a fact he'd ask me to tell you that you should never run away from your mommy again."

"Is he as big as he looks on TV?" Chrissie said.

"Bigger." Steve raised his hand over him as high as it could go.

Chrissie's eyes widened. "Wow."

Steve slid his fingers under Chrissie's chin. "So, can I tell Big Bird, you promise never to run away from mommy again?" He kept his eyes level with the blue eyes.

"I promise. You'll tell Big Bird I promised?"

"You bet I will. Now, go on home with mommy."

"Okay, Steve. Bye-bye," Chrissie said, and next to her mother, she skipped all the way to the car, her curls bouncing with her.

Her heart melting into a puddle, Emma said, "You sure have a way with children."

"How could I not? She's such a cutie." The words tapered off to a smile. "Now, how about that coffee?"

"All right, a quick one, at your place. I need to put my feet up."

Chapter 18

AFTER A BRIEF search through the car radio, Steve stopped at Boston's *More Than a Feeling*, which quickly segued into Dr. Hook sweetly asking if they could share the night together. Emma didn't think she could make it through the ride with Steve in the car. For a long while, they rode in silence.

It was a nice August night, warm, with a clear sky and a big round moon that looked almost orange. The brightness of the city lights diminished the lustre of the starlit sky, but you knew they were there.

Sidewalks were thronged with people strolling, taking the night in, and looking for good food and entertainment. Cafes and restaurant patios were alive with diners. Music streamed from each, competed and clashed. No one seemed to mind.

Traffic was light, and Steve was making all the lights. Emma rolled her window to let warm air flow in her face and breathe in the scents of the night.

"How've you been?" Steve asked, easing the car to a stop at the Stop sign.

"Okay."

Succinct with a pinch of cold shoulder, he thought. "I'm sorry I haven't…."

"It's okay." She cut him off before he could say something she'd resent him for. "I'm exhausted. Can you take me home now?"

Full chill now. This was how it was going to be, Steve thought. He asked himself why one night of sexual release had to change the dynamics of friendship? They both enjoyed it. Steve knew Emma did. As he slipped inside her, deep, deeper, Steve saw it in her face. Then, the orgasmic moans she let out told him she had. It reminded him of Coco.

Coco was a vocal one, very expressive during their lovemaking. In between her passionate moans, she'd tell him he was a fantastic lover with magical fingers and a talented mouth. Steve hadn't gone as far as to use that magic and talent on Emma. Still, whatever pent-up tension she had—and there was as much in Emma as there was in him—he'd relieved it.

The sex had been as therapeutic for Emma as it was for him, Steve reasoned, but he couldn't help and wonder why he hadn't been able to reach out to her afterward. Why had he hung up every time he started to dial her number or turned the car around when nearing Bob's?

"Are you sure you want me to drive you home?" Steve said, bringing the car to a stop on his driveway. "Please, stay for a bit, Emma. I need someone to talk to."

So do I, Emma thought, brooding for a minute before giving in to his plea.

In his basement apartment, Steve walked to the now finished kitchen, opened the refrigerator and grabbed a beer for himself and a Coke for Emma. Uncapping both, he walked them to the couch.

"Put your feet up, Emma," he said, pushing the chest closer for her reach.

"Thank you." After a short awkward silence, she said, "You've seen the wedding announcement."

Falling back into the couch next to her, Steve took a pull of his beer. "Hard not to when it's everywhere. What does she see in him, Emma? I mean, he's old enough to be her father." Steve drank deeper. "I mean, I get that he has money, and she'll probably end up in one of his movies with his help, but how could she ransom herself like that."

Ransom was a better word than the many adjectives Mary used, Emma thought.

Dependable Emma listened to Steve's jealous rant of the woman who didn't care for him. Emma bit her tongue when Steve pointed out the many letdowns Coco was in for marrying a man she didn't know or care for. Not to mention how much she was hurting him.

During his tirade, Steve never once asked Emma how she was. He didn't mention their night together. He didn't apologize for not calling afterward or any time since.

Emma didn't exist for Steve except as a sounding board, but she continued to listen without judgment.

Everyone, however, had their limit, and after thirty minutes of listening to Steve's idiotic rant, Emma reached hers and said, "Christ, Steve, Coco doesn't love Carlo. She doesn't love you. Coco loves Coco. Deal with it already." Emma watched the blood drain out of Steve's face. Realizing she misspoke, she took a quick retreat. "I'm sorry, Steve. I didn't mean it." She watched Steve put his face down in his hands. "I really am sorry, Steve."

"Don't be. You're right. I just can't shake her out of my head. I can't let go of her." His voice was barely audible.

Emma felt the same painful emotions he did, but for a very different reason. "I should go."

He caught her wrist when she got to her feet. "Don't go."

"I can't do this anymore, Steve. I can't sit here listening to you talk about Coco and pining for her." The pain in her heart made her eyes water.

"Emma. I'm sorry I've upset you. I didn't know I was." He watched her put distance between them.

"You didn't once call me after our night together. You shopped at the store on my days off. You didn't think I'd find out," she said when he glanced away. "Do you know how it makes me feel to be used as a fleeting replacement to fill your void?"

With the realization of his thoughtlessness, of the hurt he'd caused her, guilty eyes raised to her. "Jesus, I'm sorry, Emma. I didn't mean to hurt you."

"And yet you have." She drew a breath, determined to regain her calm and her dignity. "That's not all, Steve. I'm pregnant, and it's yours," she said swiftly, like ripping off a Band-Aid.

The look of fear that comes over a man told about unexpected impending fatherhood filled his face. "When? How?"

"Really, and are you kidding me?" Emma shot back. "And before you insult me, yes, I'm sure it's yours. You're the only man I've slept with—ever."

Steve raked finger through his hair. "How far along are you?"

"Eight weeks. Do the math, Steve," she snapped when his face creased into doubtful lines.

Steve paced some more, processing the news, working through it. Needing a cigarette to help him through the thought process, he shook a cigarette out of the pack in his breast pocket. Lighting it, he breathed in smoke. Panicked.

Him a father? Steve tossed the idea in his head. It terrified him, but to his surprise, in equal measure, it excited him. In seven months, there would be a boy or a little girl he created.

He wasn't sure he'd make Emma a good husband. He didn't love her, but she was a great friend and a good listener. There was no doubt in his mind Emma would make a good wife and partner. She loved him after all, of that he was sure.

Emma was right when she told him he needed to get on with his life. Coco was. And perhaps the news of Steve marrying her best friend who was pregnant with his child might get back to Coco.

With that in mind, Steve inhaled deep and said, "Let's get married, Emma." Emma's eyes went wide in shock, and she stared at Steve. "Let's have a baby together. Be my wife, Emma."

She felt her throat slam shut on her. "Are you serious?"

Steve let out a little laugh. "I am. I make a good living. I can take care of you and the baby. I have some money saved. In a couple of years, I'll have enough for a down payment on a house. What do you say, Emma?" His eyes radiated excitement over fear when he put an arm around her shoulder.

Not the down on one knee proposal she'd dreamed of, and there was no ring. There weren't the "I love you, and I want to share this journey called life with you" words or displays of emotion. It was exceptional circumstances, Emma reasoned.

She couldn't raise a child on her own or deal with her parents' disappointment when they found out she was about to become an unwed mother.

Marrying Steve to raise their child was the practical thing to do, the solution to her problems, and Emma said, "All right. Let's do it."

"We can get married at city hall next week." His lips ripe with a smile, Steve caught Emma by the waist, picked her up off her feet and spun her in the air.

The very long two months of worrying and panic washed away for Emma.

Chapter 19

MARY DROPPED THE slice of pizza in her hand on the plate and let out a whoosh of air. "Marry? Steve? Christ, Emma, it's one shock after the next with you." Mary watched Emma close the door to her bedroom when she heard Maddie racing up the stairs. "I have to stop turning down your invitations for pizza dinner. Between you and school, I'm developing an ulcer." Mary popped the Rolaids she was taking like candy now.

"You're becoming a doctor. You'll be able to take care of it." Emma's reply caused Mary to lift a brow. "Be happy for me, Mary."

"Do you understand what you're getting into with Steve?"

"I do, but I have no choice. I can't raise this baby on my own. Not to mention the disappointment I'd become for my parents if I became an unwed mother." Emma lowered the slice of pizza on her plate, wiped her lips with the napkin.

"So you'd rather risk jumping into a marriage with a man who's pining for another woman? He's going to break your heart, Emma." Mary drank water, hoping to ease her heartburn.

"He might not. He's excited about the baby. He wants to name it Jonas if it's a boy and Soledad if it's a girl. I don't know where he got the name Soledad, but I like it." Emma pinned the long white dress against her. "Do you like it? It's mom's wedding dress. She's going to alter it for me. I've asked her to remove the sleeves and add some beading around the sweetheart neckline. I know it's old, but my mom's a whiz with the sewing machine."

Seeing the excitement in Emma's eyes made Mary popped another Rolaids and set the many reasons she'd formulated against marrying Steve aside. "It's lovely. You're going to look beautiful in it. I want to give you the bridal bouquet, Emma."

"You don't have to do that, Mary. I know between tuition and books, you're strapped."

"I am strapped, but I want to. You're my best friend, and unlike Coco, I pegged you for one marriage. I'm thinking orchids. I know they're your favourite. It's not much, but...."

Tears springing to Emma's eyes, she threw her arms around her friend. "It's everything and perfect, Mary, absolutely perfect. Thank you."

"Enough of this mushy stuff." Mary pulled out of their embrace. "As a second wedding gift, I'm offering to call Coco to let her know. I know you're feeling guilty about telling her you're marrying Steve. So, if you want me to call her and invite her to the wedding, I will, but no promises. I mean, we didn't hear from her after you wrote her to tell her about your so-called 'encounter' with Steve."

"Thank you, but no. I've mailed her an invitation." Emma aimed remorseful eyes away. "Maybe, this time, she'll answer. If she doesn't, it's no big deal. I mean, we're only having a city hall wedding. We need to save our money to buy a house."

"Okay. She might surprise you and hop on that private jet of hers and fly out for your wedding."

"Fingers crossed." Emma forced a smile on her face.

Chapter 20

Fall 2002

DRESSED IN SKINNY jeans and a lilac cashmere sweater, Coco headed to the dining room for breakfast. She wasn't in the mood for her morning walk-through to greet her guests, but it was part of the drill. The meet and greet was part of the theatre that lured guests to Covington Spa. The celebrities and dignitaries who came did for the bragging rights to say they'd spent time with her at her spa.

Coco's appearances were crucial to fill the lodge's room. She was responsible for her business and employees, many of whom were townspeople employed by the spa or indirectly supported by her business. And today, Coco couldn't neglect Halle and Jennifer. She certainly couldn't overlook Michelle and Hillary.

Ordinarily, Coco enjoyed the meet and greet, but aside from the matter with Emma and Mary, she had to contend with Carlo. Today was his day, dedicated to him as she always had and always would—until death did them part. Spending time with him was a requisite of the day.

Donning the smile she didn't feel, Coco made her entrance into the dining room and stepped into the smell of coffee and expensive perfume. Guests—all women— filled the tables. The fireplace glowed with the fire that burned in the hearth.

Heads turned the moment Coco walked into the room. A-list celebrities whom Coco had worked with, produced their movies, or whom Carlo directed, greeted her. Coco made sure to stop at the table where Aline, Hillary, and Michelle debated the state of the world.

Adulation and recognition from the names in the business and VIPs were what Coco would have tripped over to get. That was in the past. These days it meant nothing to her.

Duty fulfilled, Coco scanned the dining room for Emma and Mary. She didn't expect Mary to be there but hoped reliable, forgiving Emma would be. Neither was, because of her, Coco told herself. Her egotistic, entitled ego drove her only real friends away.

Coercing Mary to keep her betrayal from Emma was the last straw. The guilt that consumed Mary for harbouring Coco's secret fractured their relationship and that with Emma. Coco was responsible for that and the reason she'd disappeared overnight.

Guilt and remorse washed over Coco at once. How did she apologize to Mary and Emma for her stupid actions when they refused to talk to her? How did she do what she must when they refused to be in the same room as her? But a way Coco had to find before it was too late.

Heaving a sigh, with the requisite smile on her face, Coco continued to make her rounds. Going from table to table, Coco greeted guests and welcomed new ones. Graciously, she posed for the requested selfies. Coco engaged in small talk before she headed out to the garden.

In the garden, at her favourite spot under the ash tree, Coco fell back onto the bench. It was the perfect fall day. A cool wind blew, and the sun gleamed gold in a clear blue sky. The pallet of fall, gold, rust, and copper painted the landscape. Coco took it all in, painted it in her mind to take with her.

Coco's eyes focused on the horizon. She thought about how perfect her life was. She had everything she wanted. At forty-one, she'd accomplished more than many in their lifetime. Her career had reached unimaginable heights before she was thirty. How could it not? The lure of glamour and fame had been irresistible. The romance of the spotlight made her set everyone and everything dear to her aside to achieve it. Her singular focus was on climbing the ladder of success, three rungs at a time and nothing, and no one was going to stop her.

She achieved incredible success. She had money, her own Learjet to whisk her to her many properties around the world. Yet, the rural spa, north of the city she hadn't called home since she left for New York, was where she felt at home.

How right Carlo was when he'd set the keys to Covington Spa in her hand and told her that in the end, we all came home.

Coco's eyes flickered to the majestic ash tree. Its canopy, ablaze in lemon yellow and apple red, spread like a giant umbrella above her. With each breeze, leaves rained around her to the ground. It was Carlo's tree. The understated plaque with the etched words *A Man's Legacy Is Limited Only By His Imagination* put a smile on her face.

Coco pulled a cigarette out of the pack and fumbled with a match. Guiltily, she lit it. She'd given up the nasty habit months ago, but lately, her shattered nerves were tightly coiled, and drinking and smoking helped her unwind.

Sucking in smoke, Coco let her thoughts wander. Until now, her life had been as perfect as it could be, but in one instant, it was turned upside down. This time, no money in the world was going to right it.

If Coco could turn the hand of time back, she would rewrite her life. The ink, however, was dry on that script, and no rewrites were allowed, only edits.

FROM THE TERRACE, EMMA'S ARMS WRAPPED around herself for warmth, she watched the tall, attractive man with the Chihuahua in tow approach Coco at the bench where she sat. He wore the spa's uniform, a tailored black suit, a white shirt and a crimson tie. Emma placed him as the man who'd checked her in. His name was Alex, and he staffed the reception desk.

It took Emma a few more seconds to put it together. Alex was the man Coco had an affair with. He was Carlo's P.A., and the affair went on right in the marital home, in the marital bed. The scandalous affair headlined the news and was the topic of conversation on every talk show and tabloid for months, leading to Coco's first movie release. The affair was said to have launched her career.

Emma saw Alex lean in to kiss Coco on both cheeks and tenderly hug her. After a short exchange, he walked to the elm tree. On the fallen leaves carpeting the ground beneath the tree, he laid the bouquet of white calla lilies in his arms.

Coco's head resting on Alex's shoulder, the dog propped on his rump beside them, they faced the tree. Afterward, taking a seat on the bench with the dog curled at their feet, Alex and Coco held hands and sat in complete silence.

Fifteen minutes passed, and Alex said something that made Coco's lips curve into a wide smile. Kissing her on the forehead, he walked away, leaving her and the dog on the bench. Curious to know what that was all about, Emma grabbed two cups of coffee and headed down the stone path to Coco.

Part II

The Middle

Sometimes we make the wrong choices for what we believe are the right reasons.

—M.L. Lexi

Chapter 21

SUMMER HAD PEAKED and fall was in the air. Two weddings, thousands of miles apart and as different as their brides were, took place on the same Saturday.

At Toronto City Hall, in a modest room with vinyl-covered banquet chairs, lined in rows of five and ten deep, where walls were devoid of art, Steve and Emma stood before the justice of the peace. Emma wore her mother's altered dress. Her hair, thanks to Mel's creativity and generosity, was artfully wrapped into a chignon. In Emma's hands, she held the bouquet of white orchids Mary gifted.

Standing on Emma's right, Steve looked handsome in a gray double-breasted suit. Mary, her maid of honour, stood on Emma's left. Maddie looked pretty in a pink tulip dress her mother created and took her flower girl role seriously. Emma's three brothers walked down the aisle giggling and shoving one another while carrying the rings tied to a heart-shaped pillow.

From the two front seats, Emma's mother fumbled in her handbag for a tissue and dabbed at her eyes as her father shot Steve a cautionary look. On the opposite side of the aisle, Steve's parents watched on with pride and relief their son chose level-headed, sensible Emma over the brash, reckless Coco.

After the ceremony, the handful of people in attendance headed to Gianna's Restaurant for dinner. At the end of the night, Steve drove Emma to the Westin Hotel for their weekend honeymoon getaway.

Emma was as happy as a bride could be.

THOUSANDS OF MILES AWAY COCO WALKED down the aisle looking stunning in the ten thousand dollar Carolina Herrera silk dress with the ten-foot monarch train. Her hair was twisted into a top knot. A tiara lined with rubies courtesy of Harry Winston "Jeweler to the Stars" held it in place. At her ears and neck, diamonds, Carlo's wedding gift to his bride-to-be, sparkled.

At the front of the church, Carlo watched Coco walk toward him with a broad smile on his tanned face. He looked handsome in the Hampton black and ivory tuxedo. His glossy, mink-coloured hair was neatly combed back.

Standing next to Carlo, his best man Alex flashed Coco a bright smile as she sashayed her way down the red aisle carpet as the four flower girls—actors hired by Alex—sprinkled white rose petals.

Every step of the way, Coco played up to the cameras like a professional. The photographs would grace the covers of newspapers and magazines and appear on television screens worldwide for everyone to see.

Coco had arrived.

After the ceremony, the celebrity couple was whisked by stretch limousine to the Bel-Air Club, where nine hundred guests were treated to a ten-course meal. There were imported wines and champagne from Italy and Spain. French cheeses, Beluga caviar, and lobsters flown from Nova Scotia for the occasion were served.

She was in her element.

Surrounded by the people she'd seen on the screen since childhood, celebrating her wedding day was a dream come true. These were her people. This was her scene. Coco was home.

Coco was as happy as a bride could be.

Chapter 22

ON COCO AND Carlo's return from their Bali honeymoon, Mark Gordon, the best acting coach in Hollywood, got to work with Coco. After her eight-hour days with Mark, Coco roped Carlo, Alex, the maid, gardener, or chauffeur, whomever she could into reading lines with her.

Determined to appear on the big screen with her husband, Coco practiced and practiced. The leading role in the *Mistress of Covington* would be hers.

When Coco wasn't with Mark, she spent her days on the set of *The Visionary*, Carlo's current movie. A keen student, Coco watched, observed, and filed everything she saw and learned in her head for future reference. Watching Carlo and his co-star deliver their lines seamlessly and on cue, Coco realized how unskilled an actor she was and how right Carlo was to rate her an okay actor.

Coco set her mind to replace the okay rating with remarkable, astounding, extraordinary.

She was Coco D'Onofrio, and although her name carried weight in Hollywood circles, she'd make sure to live up to Carlo's expectation.

THE MOMENT EMMA AND STEVE GOT home from their weekend honeymoon, life got busy. Settling into their roles as husband and wife, work, doctor appointments, and shopping for baby furniture filled their days.

The basement apartment was getting crowded, but Emma would make do. She always had. She'd never had privacy. She'd shared a room with Maddie all her life and a small home with six people. Crowding was second nature to Emma, but with Steve by her side now, everything felt like an adventure, not an inconvenience.

It was a different story for Steve. An only child, Steve revelled in his freedom and space. Married life was encroaching on his bachelor life. He felt crowded, and his freedom to come and go as he pleased was supplanted with marital responsibility.

Marriage was suffocating and cramping his style. The resentment swelled.

Then, hearing the baby's heartbeat, seeing the tiny human being he created on the ultrasound screen for the first time was transformative. Emma carried his baby, the life they made together, and Steve became the overly attentive and caring husband.

After his six-to-four workday, Steve rushed home to make dinner. By five, he was in his car on his way to pick Emma up at the end of her shift at Bob's. No way, no, how would his pregnant wife make the trek home on the bus after a long day of work.

Emma's morning sickness became so bad she couldn't hold food down or had the strength to get out of bed. It tied Steve's stomach in knots. He watched over Emma while she slept and catered to her every need.

Emma thought the tide was turning in her direction. It was a matter of time before Steve's love followed.

Steve was by her side when the abdominal pain shot through her in the middle of the night. When Emma keeled over, and her breaths became shallow a panicked, Steve picked her up and carried her to the car.

"Please slow down, Steve. The pain is easing," Emma said as Steve weaved through traffic like a madman.

"How long have you been feeling like this?"

"It's probably just indigestion. I shouldn't have had that Italian hot sausage for dinner."

"Well, we're not taking any chances." Steve kept his eyes firmly on the road when he punched the gas to make it through the changing light. "I'm taking you to St. Mike's to check out whatever is going on with you and our baby."

Our baby, Emma, heard and felt drenched in love. A warm calm descended over her and the pain dissipated. "All right, Steve. You're the boss."

"Damn straight, I am. Sit back and relax." Steve curled his hand around hers. "We'll be there in ten minutes." He punched the gas harder.

With a smile on her face, Emma closed her eyes, and her head tipped back against the headrest. She held the smile when the shocking wave of pain struck her lower abdomen harder this time. Emma remained stoic when she felt the wet discharge on her panties and smelled blood.

Chapter 23

THE JARRING PAIN, combined with the bleeding that persisted all night, resulted in a miscarriage. Emma was taken to the operating theatre in the morning, where the doctor performed a dilation and curettage to remove any remaining tissue.

"Tissue, they called it," Emma said. The hospital's smells, the ongoing exchange between patients and nurses and doctors grated on her nerves. "It's my baby." She closed her eyes against the pain of loss.

Our baby, Steve thought, and as numb as he felt, as much as he needed consoling himself, he didn't correct Emma. She was reacting out of the pain of loss, he told himself. Then there was the physical pain she'd endured all night. It was making her physically and mentally tired and her mind hazy. Under those circumstances, anyone would misconstrue words and actions, and he held his words.

When Steve remained silent, Emma closed her eyes and slid into her despair.

Emma remained hospitalized for three days. Steve stayed by her side the entire time. He said little because nothing he'd say would bring his baby back.

On the fourth day, a numb Steve helped his wife to the car. In complete silence, he drove her home.

Emma set her teary eyes out the car window. Unlike her mood, the day was bright and clear. Heads bent against the chilly fall wind, everyone went about their business. University students headed to class. Men and women, briefcases in hand, rushed to offices in tall buildings. Street cleaners kept order while children played in the park. Everyone went about their day, their everyday life.

But it wasn't a typical day for Emma. She'd lost her baby, the living being growing inside of her for the past ten weeks. They told her it was a girl, which worsened the hurt when flashes of the what-could-have-been rolled in her head.

She was broken. Her heart was broken.

Resting her forehead against the car window, Emma let the tears flow. When Emma started to sob, Steve kept his eyes firmly on the road ahead. He hadn't slept since he brought Emma into the hospital and was exhausted, heartbroken and feared saying the wrong thing. Emma was too fragile.

Steve hoped Mary would know what to do and how to deal with Emma.

TO STEVE'S RELIEF MARY WAS WAITING for them at home.

The moment they walked in, Mary threw her arms around Emma. "I'm so sorry. Are you all right? Are you feeling okay? Come sit down." Mary walked Emma to the couch. "Steve, make Emma a cup of tea. Chamomile if you have it." Mary tilted her head toward the kitchen, a gesture to make himself scarce. "Have a lie-down, Emma."

"I don't want to lie down, Mary. I've been in bed for three days." Irritation edged into Emma's voice.

"Fine, sit and relax then. Tea, Steve," Mary urged when he remained watching on.

"Stop fussing, Mary, and I don't want tea. What I want is my baby. It was a girl. That's what they said." Emma's voice dropped to a whisper.

"I'm sorry, Emma." Mary put a supportive hand on Emma's shoulder.

"A little girl. We were going to name her Soledad." Big silent tears coursed down Emma's face.

At the kitchen stove, emotion choked Steve, and he dropped the teakettle on the burner. His eyes on Emma, he thought she looked so small, so broken. It shattered him. It was too much for one man to handle. Slipping his hands in his pockets, Steve shifted to look anywhere but at Emma.

"Umm, we don't, umm, have chamomile," Steve said, sniffing. "I'll go to the supermarket to pick some up."

Mary watched him nervously scan the room for the car keys. "They're on the counter in front of you, Steve," Mary said. "Take your time."

"Okay. Sure. Thanks." Steve hurried out the front door.

"You've had substantial blood loss. You'll feel the chills for some time." Mary reached for the plaid throw on the chair and wrapped it around her shoulders when the quick chill ran through Emma's body, and she shivered.

"To have a baby, a family is all I've ever wanted, Mary."

"I know." Mary set the glass of water in Emma's hand. "Drink. You need to keep hydrated."

"Why can't I have one thing I want? Just one." Emma sipped when Mary gestured to do so. "I don't ask for much."

"Don't think about anything, Emma. Right now, you need to relax." She dug a tissue from the box and handed it to Emma.

"I've lost my baby, and Steve will probably leave me now."

"Why would you say that? He was by your bedside the entire time. He's a man. He was confused. He needed someone to talk to," Mary explained when the frown creased Emma's brow.

"I was in a vulnerable position. Anyone would have been supportive."

"Stop overthinking, Emma. You're going to drive yourself crazy."

"Don't you think I don't know that the only reason he married me was that I was pregnant? I just figured I had enough love for the two of us, and eventually, he'd fall into love with me, but now that I killed his baby, he has no reason to stay with me."

Feeling the pain and the overwhelming demand of womanhood Emma felt, Mary's tears wanted to come, but she blinked them away. "You did not kill your baby, Emma."

"It's my body. I did this. I worked too many hours on my feet all day. I didn't exercise. I stayed at a physically stressful job, but we needed the money. I rushed through the ten-minute lunches and didn't eat properly. I...."

Mary cut off Emma's emotional rant. "What happened to you is out of your control. It's your body's way of signalling," chromosomal abnormalities in the fetus, she stopped short of saying the medical term Emma wouldn't appreciate in her vulnerable state of mind. "It's nature, Emma. It's nothing to do with you. Do you understand that? Answer me, Emma," Mary urged when she sensed Emma's fragility and feared what she might do.

"I understand. I do, but it doesn't feel that way right now."

"I know, but you'll overcome this and come out stronger. And you'll get pregnant again when you and your body are ready."

Emma shrugged her shoulders. "I don't know if Steve will want to."

Chapter 24

READING THE LAST line from the script, in her newly schooled British accent, Coco couldn't have been happier to see the brimming smile on Carlo's face. "Is that the look of approval?"

"She's worked very hard to get here, Carlo." Alex rose from the couch and crossed the milk-white Talavera tile to the terrace doors.

Music from cicadas tangling with the sound of wind and water poured into the living room the moment he pushed the doors open. Bright stars and a round moon painted the night sky and sailed white over calm waters.

In the distance, Alex made out a group of teenagers gathered around a bonfire enjoyed the night. The faint strumming of *Hotel California* from an acoustic guitar floated along with laughter.

"It shows. You've improved loads in the six months I've been away on location." Carlo leaned in, gave Coco a congratulatory peck on the cheek.

"She's a fast learner. She even has the British accent down perfectly." Alex rounded the bar, reached for three balloon glasses and the cognac bottle. "A few more weeks, and she'll be ready."

"I concur." Carlo had on chinos, a white polo shirt, and tan loafers.

"You think so?" Words tumbled out of Coco in excitement as she fell into the buttery-soft cushion of the living room couch with Carlo.

"I know so." Carlo flashed Coco a smile. You keep at it. No distractions, and continue to focus on your acting and vocal lessons, and you'll be ready for the part." He stretched out his legs, his feet comfortably crossed at the ankles.

"Carlo's one hundred percent right, Coco." Alex poured cognac into the three glasses and walked them to the couch. "No distractions."

"Promise. No distractions," Coco said and meant it.

Coco had a disciplined mind. She could set her focus solely on the one thing if she wanted it badly enough. And for the past six months, her mind revolved around her training and nothing else.

Coco set aside every distraction that could derail her. Sex, shopping, clubbing, and reading Mary's letters were put by to ensure her mind stayed focused on what was important. Mary was a downer, always infusing her logic into life. Coco didn't need that type of negativity in her life right now. Mary's five unopened letters were tucked far back on the top shelf of Coco's bedroom closet—out of sight, out of mind.

The first of Mary's letters came before her wedding, which Coco assumed was an apology she neither wanted nor needed. If Mary and Emma were proper friends, they would have accepted Coco's invitation to the wedding from the onset and stood by her side at the altar.

But they weren't there on her wedding day, and she wasn't about to entertain their feeble penned apology. She didn't need them or the mental gymnastics Mary's judgement put her through, especially not now. Coco had more important things to focus on.

"I'll talk to my director first thing tomorrow morning and start the ball rolling. I want to take a few weeks to rest up from my last shoot, but we'll begin right afterward."

Coco's face glowed. "I'll be ready to audition when you give the go."

"Honey, you won't have to audition to get the part." Alex offered a glass to Coco and Carlo.

"I don't want charity. I want to earn it." Carlo, the savage critics, or viewers, would not label Coco an "okay" actor—no way, no how. "I will audition for this part and get it fair and square. Understood?" Determined eyes on Carlo, Coco took a sip of cognac.

"No charity. This is my movie. I'm financing it, and Mark has been preparing you for the role since the beginning. And he told me you're almost ready to take on the role. After seeing what you did just now, I concur with Mark." Carlo lifted his glass in half-salute.

Coco stopped her drinking mid-sip. She wasn't sure whether to feel irritation or joy. The latter won out because why inject negativity into a perfect moment. "Why didn't you tell me?"

Matching the gleam in Coco's eyes, Carlo said, "No, distractions, Mistress Cordelia Covington." Carlo spaced each word for effect.

"Mistress Cordelia Covington." Coco let the words flow musically.

THOUSANDS OF MILES AWAY, FEELING HELPLESS against Emma's rising hysteria, Steve kept his words soothing as he walked alongside the gurney on her way into surgery.

Emma never imagined their life steering toward the normal of married life after her miscarriage, but it had. Steve didn't express the love Emma hoped for, but the fact he stayed by her side told her it was a matter of time. The fact Steve was the one who suggested they try for another baby told Emma it was a matter of time before he came around.

There was some nudging, with a pinch of trickery on Emma's part. What man didn't need female prodding? In the end, when the doctor confirmed she was eight weeks pregnant, Steve rode on the thrill with her.

The doctor assured them a pregnancy that followed a miscarriage stood a good chance to carry to term. Ecstatic by the news, Emma and Steve pulled the baby clothes and crib out of storage. They picked names Aiden for a boy and Hope for a girl.

One night after work, Steve surprised Emma with a baseball glove. "Oiled and ready for use when Aiden, or Hope, was ready to throw the ball around at the nearby park," he told Emma.

Walking alongside the gurney into the emergency room, Steve felt impotent with Emma's blood staining the sheets. His heart broke for the second time in months for her and him.

He'd have to store the baby clothes and crib away before Emma came home. You think he'd learn or at least listen to Mary when she told them to hold off pulling the baby things out of storage until Emma crossed into her second trimester. You'd think Steve would learn from their first experience when Emma spiralled into depression after her miscarriage.

Emma tried to hide her hurt, but he could see it clearly in her eyes. As broken as Emma was from their first loss six months ago, she was the perfect, devoted, hardworking wife. How could he not give her the baby she wanted?

"You're in good hands, Emma," Steve said when the shocking pain poured out of her.

Emma gripped his hand as he started to step away.

"I'm not going anywhere. I'll be right here when you come out." Steve gave her hand a squeeze of reassurance.

Chapter 25

"THAT'S WHAT HE said, Mary, and sure enough, when I came out of the anesthesia, Steve was right there by my bedside," Emma said once Mary encouraged Steve and her boyfriend to leave Emma's hospital room and go in search of a cup of coffee.

"He's devoted to you, Emma," Mary forced herself to say. Mary saw through Steve's plan to have a child with Emma, hoping it would get back to Coco. What he planned to gain by the scheme was anyone's guess because it wouldn't bring Coco back. "How are you feeling?"

Understanding Mary's question was about her mental state Emma said, "I don't want to talk about me." She carefully shifted her achy body on the bed. "So, Adam Tyrell. He's hunky, Mary."

Medium height and radiating intelligence from the eyes as dark as ink, Adam Tyrell was precisely the type of man Emma expected to catch Mary's eye. His short hair was as black as his eyes. The body beneath the pale blue shirt and jeans was trim. He carried himself with the poise and sophistication of the doctor he aimed to become.

"He is, isn't he?"

"Where'd you meet him?"

Mary propped an additional pillow behind Emma. "He's in a few of my classes. He's leaning toward a specialization in oncology. When I told him I was coming to see you, he volunteered to drive me. He can't seem to get enough of hospitals, the smell, the daily clatter, and the beeping machines."

Adam ticked all the boxes, thought Emma. He was Mary's perfect match. "You've met your dream, man."

Mary gave Emma a slow smile. "It's early days. We've only been dating for a few weeks, and I haven't decided if I'm keeping him around."

Both women snorted a laugh, causing Emma to cringe when the pain speared from her lower belly. "Don't make me laugh, Mary."

"Sorry. Now, never mind Adam. Going back to what you said about Steve being there for you. He's your husband, Emma and the father of your child." Mary's eyes melted into sympathy. "I'm sorry about the miscarriage, and I don't want to put more on you than you're already dealing with, but he also lost a baby."

Emma's tired eyes met Mary's, and the tears spilled.

"Men don't know how to express their feelings, and Steve is no exception. He's hurting for the child you lost as much as you are." Mary wandered over to the window, cracked it open a notch to let spring air into the room.

"I know." Emma closed her eyes again.

"I've always spoken my mind, and I'm going to do it now. I appreciate what you had to do to get Steve to agree to try for the second baby, but nothing you do will stop him from thinking of Coco and making you feel ... hopeless," was the best word Mary could come up with. "Steve will always be in love with Coco. It's a fact you need to come to terms with."

It was true enough. Still, Emma shot back, "Don't hold back, Mary," out of guilt, anger, pain. She wasn't sure.

Now Mary's brows shot up. "What I say is out of love. Steve thinks he's in love with Coco because he can't have her. It's not a guy thing. It's how human beings are built. But you're not built like Coco. You can't do what she does best. What you need to do is mourn with him, Emma. Mourn together for the child you've lost. It will bring you closer together than any stunt you instigate. An act of love, not duplicity, will draw him close to you." Mary left Emma, mulling the thought over in her head.

MARY'S WORDS LEFT EMMA THINKING. AS much as she didn't think she could give Steve more love than she already did, Emma concluded Mary was right. Her duplicity was likely to push Steve away.

Emma didn't want to lose Steve or her hope for a family with him. She'd do anything to prevent that from happening. And she did.

Emma mourned with Steve. She talked with him, not at him as she had after her first miscarriage. She listened, not dismissed him as the father whose sole contribution ended after a roll in the sheets.

Once again, rational Mary was right. Steve hurt as much as Emma hurt. Steve cried with her and needed to be held and comforted as much as she did.

"What do you say to plant an apple tree in the backyard for our baby?" Emma spooned drained spaghetti onto two dishes and topped them with sauce.

"That sounds like a good idea." Steve set forks, wine bottle, and glasses on the table.

"Check with your parents to make sure they're okay with the idea?" Emma grated parmesan over each spaghetti dish.

"I'm sure they are. I'll ask them just the same." Steve slid one of the glasses he poured wine into across the table.

"We can have a sort of ceremony." Emma scraped the chair next to Steve's back and sat. "We can ask Mary and Adam, your parents, and mine, and Father Domenic to give a blessing."

That brought him unexpected comfort, and Steve reached to cover her hand. "All right. Let's do it this weekend."

Emma fell into a brief silence. "I'm sorry, Steve."

"Why? What for?" Steve brought a forkful of rolled spaghetti to his mouth.

"For the miscarriages. I'm sorry for putting you through them."

Steve's eyes rose to meet Emma's face. "It's not your fault."

"It's my body doing this. It's me causing the miscarriages."

Steve cupped her chin, raised her face until her swimming eyes met his. "You're not the cause of anything. It's ... nature at work." Mary told him that, and it was the best he could say.

"I know how much you want children." Her breath hitched. "I'd understand if you want to walk away from this, from me."

The statement disarmed him as much as the tears flowing from her eyes. Steve brushed his lips to hers. "You can't get rid of me that easily."

"But...."

"But nothing. We'll try again, Emma."

She took a moment to wrap her brain around that. "Really?"

Steve nodded. "When we're both ready, we'll try again."

"Really?"

"Yes, really."

Floating in the warmth of the emotions overflowing in her, Emma said, "I love you, Steve."

He sent her a quick smile. "Eat up before it gets cold," he said, twisting spaghetti onto his fork.

Chapter 26

UNDER A SUN-WASHED summer day in Hampshire, England, Coco squeezed her eyes shut and opened them. She wasn't dreaming. She was in the midst of a movie set at Highclere Castle, the chosen location for *The Mistress of Covington.*

The movie set was a buzz of activity. There were tents and trailers. The largest trailer on the lot had her and Carlo's names on the door.

Soldiers outfitted in the British khaki uniforms worn in WWI practiced their lines and handling of prop weapons. Automobiles typical of the period lined the gravel driveway: a 1924 Cadillac, a convertible 1927 AC Six, along with the many others Coco would get the privilege to ride in with Carlo, her leading man. Background actors in black and white livery with tails or long-skirt maid uniforms mingled under striped tents at the long buffet tables.

Coco wore a gray, notch-collar jacket, with a white lace blouse, and a floor-length skirt. Elbow high satin gloves covered her hands, and a black felt Victorian cloche hat topped the classic vintage twenties look. Coco looked every bit the seductive mistress she was to play.

Coco took a moment to settle the nerves churning in her stomach when she saw what appeared like hundreds of cameras. All would be focused on her every move, her every gesture, her every mistake, missed cues, and missteps. To top it off, the cameras were going to add ten pounds.

She tossed the glazed donut in her hand into the garbage.

Feeling the sudden sinking sensation in the pit of her stomach, she debated why she got into the business.

Breathe, Coco, breathe.

"Don't be nervous. You're ready for this." In a striped herringbone suit, a white shirt with a club collar, and a bowler hat, Carlo looked striking as the handsome philandering Lord Covington.

"I think I just forgot every line of my dialogue." Coco took the bottle of water Carlo offered.

"I doubt that, and it's good to be nervous. It'll push you that much harder to perfect your role." Carlo reached for her hand. "I'll be alongside you every step of the way. I am the man you're about to have a torrid affair with." Coco laughed at that and felt her uneasiness wane. "Feel better?"

"I do, my Lord," Coco said in the inflection of the privileged British class and leaned in to brush her lips to his.

"At your service, my slutty Lady."

Coco hooted a laugh. "I am a woman of loose morals but a well-rounded professional." Coco lifted her hand to rest on his cheek. "Thank you for this, Carlo. For making a dream, I started to give up on, a reality."

"There's nothing to thank me for. Besides, you're going to make it up to me when you get nominated for an Oscar, and the movie becomes a worldwide sensation."

Her stomach was tied into knots again. "An Oscar? Worldwide sensation? Jesus, no pressure there."

"My lovely wife, that's not at all what I meant. What I mean by that is that you're that good an actor, and I wouldn't be surprised if you end up with, in the least, an Oscar nomination."

"I wish I felt as confident as you." Coco and Carlo turned in the direction of Alex's voice. Clipboard in hand, Fredo trailed at his feet. Behind Fredo, Aunt Abby and Mrs. Carter in colourful, willowy summer dresses and wide-brimmed hats eyed every uniformed man that walked past them.

"You guys finally made it." Coco leaned in to hug Aunt Abby and Mrs. Carter and crouched down to kiss Fredo on the head.

"What am I, chopped liver?" Alex offered a cheek for Coco to peck, which she did and followed it with a tight hug.

"I save the best for last," she whispered in his ear.

"Mmm-hmm. We came straight from the airport, and by the way, you look fabulous," Alex said, drawing her back, far enough to look at her with an analytical eye.

"Makeup and wardrobe know their craft well." Coco scooped Fredo off the ground into her arms. "I've missed you, buddy."

"Sorry we're late, but I was working on the press release and promo for the movie launch. You'll start seeing them in print and broadcast media this afternoon. I think you'll be pleased. Before I forget, this came for you. It's from Mary." Coco took the envelope Alex held out. "It arrived a month ago. I'm sorry for the delayed delivery. I wanted to deliver it in person. Aren't you going to read it?" he asked when she tucked it into her skirt pocket.

"Not right now. Mary is a downer, and I need my full focus right now. Carlo thinks I can snatch myself an Oscar."

"Well, you are playing a slutty mistress."

Coco gave Alex a little shove. "Based on that, I should be nominated for several Oscars."

"If I know Carlo, he'll take them any way they come. You know actors will prostitute themselves for ego strokes." Alex linked his arm with Coco's and followed Carlo as he started toward their personalized director chairs.

"Alex knows me well. But Coco will earn her awards the traditional way." Carlo hopped up onto his chair, picked up the scripts on the table next to it and handed one to Coco. "Shooting starts in an hour. Let's run through our lines one last time and get you that Oscar."

FOR TWELVE MONTHS, COCO BREATHED AND lived the life of Cordelia Covington—even when off-camera. When she wasn't in front of the cameras, Coco spent her time reading her lines for Mark Gordon, Carlo, and Alex. Their critique was invaluable to Coco, who wouldn't settle for anything less than perfection.

Filming ahead of schedule, Alex approved the press junket for rollout. Press releases, television, radio, and billboard advertising campaigns were launched. Interviews with major television shows and journalists to create buzz around the film were set in motion.

Coco was everywhere.

STEVE SAW COCO ON MAGAZINE COVERS, in the entertainment section of newspapers. There were commercials every hour on the hour on all the major stations promoting her upcoming movie. Billboards fourteen feet high and forty-eight feet wide displayed her and Carlo in a tight embrace.

Steve had set Coco to the back of his mind to make his marriage with Emma work, but seeing her everywhere, sparked his need for her. Steve couldn't shake her from his system. He wanted more than he'd ever wanted her.

Chapter 27

Fall 2002

EMMA WALKED UP to the bench where Coco remained after Alex went back to the lodge. "Hi." She thought she saw Coco wipe tears from her eyes before she turned and flashed her a forced smile. Dark circles under her eyes stood out stark against her fair skin. "You haven't given up the nasty habit."

Coco pitched the cigarette on the grass. "It's too late for me to change. I'm too old and too set in my ways. Is one of those for me?"

Emma handed her one of the cups in her hands. "I saw you sitting out here and thought you could use a warm cup of coffee."

"Thank you. I came out here when I didn't find you or Mary in the dining room." Coco wrapped her hands around the cup for warmth.

"It's so peaceful here. I slept deeply and well all night and didn't wake until nine this morning. I only came down a few minutes ago."

"Mary slept in too?"

"She must have gone for a run. She took it up in medical school as part of her healthier living kick," Emma explained when Coco looked at her with a puzzled expression.

There was so much Coco didn't know about her friends anymore, she thought and wished she could get the opportunity to spend more time with them.

"My guess this morning's run is to relieve stress as much as maintain her routine. Mary was rather worked up after our conversation."

"I know. You figure, amongst us, I was the one with the flair for the dramatic," Coco said, eliciting a smile. "I promised I'd tell you everything once Aunt Abby gets here later today, and I will. She's bringing with her the reason I brought us together this weekend."

"I believe you." Emma surveyed Coco with eyes that took in every detail of her drained appearance. "Are you all right, Coco? You're not wearing any makeup." Coco threw back her head and laughed. The first time in a long time, she'd had a good laugh. "I don't think I've ever seen you without makeup. You look a little washed out without it."

"I can always count on you for a good laugh, Emma." Coco laughed louder. "It's the healthy, makeup-free look I'm now promoting at the spa, but I'll keep it in mind. This is Fredo II," Coco said when the dog looked up at Emma with his big brown eyes.

"As in *The Godfather's* Fredo," Emma said, delighting the dog with head scratches.

Coco nodded. "Carlo named him. He's not particularly bright, but he's loyal."

"And adorable." Emma's eyes followed Fredo as he strolled toward the tall grass and disappeared.

"He's off to do his thing." Coco signalled Emma to take the seat next to her.

"What does the plaque mean, Coco?" Emma watched Coco roll hesitant eyes to the tree and back at her. "Sorry, I don't mean to intrude. You don't have to tell me if you don't want to."

Trust was part of the healing. "It's where Carlo's ashes are buried along with the first Fredo. No one but Alex, Fredo II, and now you know. It's what Carlo wanted. The biggest showman on earth wanted the least amount of attention after death."

Emma read about Carlo's death in the papers. The reported cause was a heart attack, but the doubters didn't believe that to be the true reason. The articles and the speculation intensified when Coco refused to hold the funeral with the pomp and pageantry expected for a celebrity of Carlo's popularity. Speculation grew when she refused to disclose his burial site. To this day, his diehard fans combed Hollywood for his grave. And here he was thousands of miles from Hollywood, in a nondescript, small town in Northern Ontario.

"My wonderful, loving husband's wish is to rest in peace after his death, and I'm going to do my best to ensure his wish is met. Please understand this is what Carlo wanted," was the quote that appeared in the papers.

Coco's devotion to Carlo and her thoughtfulness surprised Emma then as much as it did now. Not the Coco she knew, and Emma's respect for her grew tenfold.

"And today is the anniversary of his death," Emma remembered.

Coco nodded. "Alex, a good friend of Carlo's who works here, and I memorialize this day every year. We grieve in the understated manner in which Carlo wanted by laying his favourite flowers at the foot of this tree and saying a silent prayer together. No matter what you may have heard or read in the tabloids, I loved Carlo."

Coco's compassion moved Emma. To see the grieving woman she saw before her surprised and touched Emma. "Your secret's safe with me, Coco."

"Thank you, Emma." Coco closed her eyes when she felt the throbbing headache expanding inside her skull.

"Are you all right?"

"Yes, I am. I just have a headache coming on."

Emma met Coco's eyes with a long, unfathomable stare. "Why is Mary so angry with you, Coco? Does it have anything to do with her disappearing from my life a decade ago? You disappeared long ago, but Mary hadn't, not until you reappeared. I can't help to think it's connected." There was no anger in Emma's voice, only the need for answers. "What are we doing here, Coco? Why have you brought us together now?"

Coco crouched down to pick up Fredo when he appeared through the tall grass and meandered back to her. "I've made mistakes, Emma. Mistakes I need to correct." Coco's eyes focused on some distant point, she scratched Fredo's head.

"We've all made mistakes, Coco. I … I've made mistakes."

"That may be, Emma, but yours didn't hurt people."

The pang of guilt drove Emma to say what had been eating at her all these years, "I got pregnant with Steve's baby not long after you left. I wrote you a letter to tell you but trashed it," she spewed in quick succession. The tension, the guilt, the remorse weighing her down all these years vanished.

Coco could only stare at Emma. "Why did you trash it?"

"Would you have been pleased to hear I was carrying Steve's child?"

Coco felt sick to her stomach. "Christ."

"Christ is right."

"How did it happen?

Emma's brows furrowed. "Really?"

"You know what I mean."

Emma laid out her reason for why she ended up at Steve's door and what followed. "A few weeks later, I found out I was pregnant."

Overcome by Emma's story, the sick feeling began to stir in Coco's gut. Part shame, part regret, and part anger at herself intensified. She'd stolen Emma's life, Steve's life, to fill the temporary void in her life.

Coco looked pointedly at Emma. "I'm sorry, Emma. I'm so sorry."

Emma looked shocked. "It's me who should be apologizing."

"You?"

"I married the man you were involved with for four years. Friends don't do that."

Jesus! Coco shook her head. "I didn't know you were in love with Steve. I thought... It doesn't matter what I thought. I'm sorry I overlooked your feelings for Steve. Had I not been so focused on me and my needs, I would have been more aware and stepped aside." Visibly distraught, Coco felt the pain of her betrayal, the shame for her disloyalty to a friend who wanted nothing but friendship from her.

Stunned with shock, Emma said, "Would you have stepped aside, Coco?"

There was no turning back now.

We are who we are, Coco, though. All she could do now was earn Emma and Mary's friendship and trust again by showing them how much she needed and loved them. Love was the glue that bound human beings together, and Coco hoped it would do that when she set her plan in motion. Coco hoped her plan would right every wrong she'd committed.

She had to do it soon. Time was running out.

Chapter 28

Winter 1982

EMMA BLEW OUT a breath, fluttering the stray strands of her hair off her face. Clearing the single car garage of years of accumulated keepsakes was the last step to claim the red brick bungalow Steve's parents turned over to Steve and her when they moved to Florida.

The house's interior, which hadn't been updated in decades, thanks to Steve's construction expertise, had already undergone a makeover. Parquet floors were restored to their original shine, and Green walls were painted a sexy metallic blue. On newly replaced windows, lace curtains hung. In the kitchen, there were now white porcelain tiles with blue-gray streaks in place of faded linoleum. Cupboards were refurbished, and appliances replaced with modern white ones. It reflected her and Steve's taste.

In the summer, Emma would put her touch on the small garden bordering the house. It would be her biggest challenge, but Emma would give it a go. Emma was determined to have the homey place she'd always wanted for her and Steve.

The garage door was closed to keep the winter cold out. From inside the garage, Emma heard the roar of a passing car, the bark of a dog followed. Dust motes floated like snowflakes in the ribbons of light from the fixture Steve installed on the garage roof. A soulful R&B

tune flowed from Emma's portable radio set on the garbage can's lid.

Emma slid her eyes over to Maddie, who'd volunteered to help clean out the garage. Maddie had on sneakers, jeans, and a pink turtleneck sweater. All hand me down from Emma's youth. She'd tied a red, plaid scarf around her dark curls to hold them back just like her big sister.

"Zip up your jacket, Maddie. Mom will kill me if you catch a cold," Emma said.

"Okay." Zipped up, Maddie rummaged through the Bankers box she found in the corner of the garage under the blue tarp. "Do you think we'll see Coco again, Emma?"

"Be careful, Maddie, don't go hurting yourself, or Mom will have my head." Emma dodged.

"She won't because I'll blame it on the triplets. I blame everything on them." Maddie's wicked, dimpled grin made Emma smile.

"That's not very nice."

"They're always in trouble, so it makes no difference. Boys." Maddie hissed. "Can you at least get me Coco's autograph?"

"I don't know. She's very busy." Emma tossed old paint cans into a black garbage bag.

"Will you try? Everyone in school thinks I'm lying when I tell them I know her. They don't believe me when I say she's your best friend. It'd be so good to prove Judy Epstein so wrong. She thinks she's so smart and knows everything." Maddie reached into the box and pulled out the following photo album.

"What have I told you about people like Judy?"

"That they act that way because they're insecure. Still, I want to prove her so wrong." Maddie glanced over her shoulder with narrowed eyes. "Coco looks so pretty in her poster. Don't you think so?"

"Why all the sudden interest in Coco? What made you think of her?" Maddie held up the poster of Coco. "Where did you get that?"

"In this box. There are lots of pictures of her in here." Crossing to Maddie, Emma's big blue eyes puzzled when she looked down.

The box was full of Coco. Coco's green eyes smiled up at Emma from the cover of People magazine, Vanity Fair, US Weekly, and the many others featuring her in the past months. Eyes full with hurt, Emma pulled the tarp back and uncovered the additional three boxes. Flipping through the collection of photo albums in the boxes, Emma couldn't believe what she saw. There were hundreds of clipped newspaper articles, magazine covers, and photographs of Coco promoting her movie.

"I can't believe you know such a famous person," Maddie said, handing Emma the stack of photographs of Coco bound with an elastic band. "You have to get me her autograph, Emma. If I showed it to Judy, I'd prove to her and everyone I wasn't lying. Will you get it for me, Emma? Please."

"Yeah. Sure, I'll ask her for an autograph when I write to her to let her know I'm pregnant," Emma said when her brain cleared. "You're going to be an auntie, Maddie."

"You said that the last two times."

Emma blinked back the tears springing to her eyes. "I feel it in my bones that this time it will happen, Maddie. You will be an auntie."

There was something so sad resonating in Emma. It compelled Maddie to hug her big sister tightly. "I really, really hope you're a girl. Boys are stinky." Maddie aimed the comment at Emma's tummy. "Make her be a girl, Emma."

"I'll see what I can do." Emma heard the tears in her voice and cleared her throat to disguise them. "For now, I need you to promise me we'll keep the secret of these boxes between us. Promise me, Maddie, you won't say anything to anyone about them." Emma covered the boxes and set them back under the tarp.

"I promise." Maddie's face went brilliant with a smile when she heard Steve call out from inside the house. "Steve's home from work."

Emma caught Maddie's arm when she turned to run into the house. "Remember, Maddie, not a word."

"I promised already. I was going to tell him how good an aunt I'm going to be. I can tell him about the baby, right?"

"You can," Emma said, wondering how Steve was going to take the news.

Chapter 29

AT EMMA'S OAK kitchen table, Mary dropped into a chair. "Christ, Emma," she muttered in disbelief.

The smells of brewed coffee and Pine-Sol hung in the air. Except for a coffee maker and a bamboo bowl topped with fresh fruit, the kitchen counters were clear of clutter. Appliances and tiled floor sparkled clean. The place gleamed. On the facing wall, two framed prints of black-spotted cows hung. Their names were Petunia and Mable. Sunlight streamed from the newly installed sliding door leading to the backyard deck, lighting the room bright.

"How do you propose getting around telling Steve you're not pregnant when the time comes?"

"I'm hoping to get pregnant by then."

Baffled eyes looked up to Emma. "Jesus, Emma, Steve's not a mathematician, but I think he can do simple math. What possessed you to pull a stunt like this?"

Silently, Emma walked two cups of coffee to the kitchen table and sat across Mary.

"You lied to Maddie."

"She'll get over it," Emma snapped with an impatient huff. Why did Mary always have to be so critical? She was fighting for her marriage, and all Mary could do was point out fault.

"Maddie," Mary repeated to drive her point home. "An impressionable girl who looks up to her big sister."

Heaving a sigh, Emma passed a hand over her face. "I know."

"Why, Emma? Why would you do such a thing?"

Twisting the ring on her finger, Emma proceeded to tell Mary about the boxes Maddie found in the garage. "They were chock full of Coco. He's been collecting articles, magazines, and everything in between for months. When he was in bed with me, he was probably thinking of her. I know what I did was wrong, but it was a trigger reaction."

Mary bit back the words at the tip of her tongue. Laying out the facts, stating the obvious to someone blinded by love was as helpful as dousing a fire with gasoline. As much as Emma knew deep down Steve was and would always be in love with Coco and only Coco, hope was an eternal spring for Emma. The trials of love and devotion, Mary thought.

"Christ, I'm so stupid. I've messed everything up." Emma dropped her head on folded arms.

Mary closed her hand over Emma's arm. "We'll figure something out."

Emma raised her head. "You do take 'we support one another no matter what,' to heart."

"I do."

"You're a true friend, Mary. I'm glad to have you in my life."

"Ditto." Mary wrapped her left hand around her coffee cup, and as she brought it to her lips, Emma saw it.

It was a modest size, and it was on her engagement finger. "Mary, are you engaged?" Emma watched Mary's smile widen as she stared at her ringed finger. "You are, and here I am, as usual, going on and on about me. Adam promised you a ring on his graduation from medical school, and he came through. I'm so happy for you, Mary." Emma drew Mary into a sisterly hug. "You know Adam is perfect for you."

"He is, isn't he?" Mary heard herself say.

"When did it happen? Did he get down on bended knee? Have you set a date? How do I address you, Mrs. or Dr. Adam Tyrell? Are you going to live together? God, I have so many questions."

"Firstly, I will be known as Dr. Mary Carter, and it happened Monday. He took me out for pizza at our favourite place near the campus. He didn't get down on one knee. You know the bacteria on public floors can manifest into so many infectious diseases." Mary pointed out, and Emma thought how perfect she and Adam were together. "And no, we haven't set a date yet, but we're moving in together. There's lots of time for the tying the knot thing yet. Right now, I want to stay focused on my studies, and Adam wants to concentrate on his career. We can't derail our objective."

Yeah, they were soulmates, Emma thought. "Do you want me to write to Coco to let her know?"

Mary's five letters to Coco going unanswered, she said, "She's busy with the launch of her film. I'll write to her when Adam and I set a date." Maybe.

Chapter 30

THE SCANDAL HEADLINED the six o'clock news. It was the feature story in all the news, tabloids, newspapers, and magazines. The photographs were grainy, but you could make out Coco, and Carlo's right-hand man, Alex, in a tight embrace, their lips locked in a passionate kiss.

There was speculation, so much speculation.

The paparazzo who took the photographs was alleged to have sold them to the highest bidder for one hundred thousand dollars.

Many were sympathetic to Carlo, who'd been a supportive, loving husband. The man had gone as far as financing *The Mistress of Covington* to allow his young, manipulative, money-grabbing wife to fulfill her dream, said some.

Those on Team Coco couldn't blame her for seeking comfort in the arms of the handsome assistant who was there when Carlo left his newlywed wife for months to film his next film. A virile, beautiful woman like Coco had needs.

Regardless of whom fans supported, all enjoyed the novella-like overtones of Carlo and Coco D'Onofrio's life playing out in the public eyes. Like predators in the wild, people hungered to hear more of the eyebrow-raising scandalous affair that went on under Carlo's nose, in his home and bed, with his money. Newspapers and magazines circulation blew up, and television ratings shot through the roof.

Mrs. Carter, who wasn't as liberal-minded as Aunt Abby was, couldn't bite her tongue and had a stern talk with Coco when she saw the report break.

"How could you do this to Carlo?" Mrs. Carter chastised while Aunt Abby's eyebrows raised evenly.

She was Mary's aunt, cut from the same cloth, Coco thought. "Mrs. C...."

Mrs. Carter cut Coco off. "The man has been nothing but loving, kind, and generous to you, Coco. For Christ's sake, he gave your aunt, who all of a sudden has lost her tongue, and me his credit card so we could get ourselves a travelling wardrobe."

"I...."

Aunt Abby cut Coco off this time. "And you sure got your money's worth, didn't you, you old biddy?" Aunt Abby pointed out.

"Didn't the man say he wanted me to look my best for the trip?" Mrs. Carter countered.

"It's a far walk off that pier," Aunt Abby shot back.

"Jealousy will get you nowhere," Mrs. Carter snapped.

"Pfft, as if. Did you need to buy that five hundred dollar hat on the man's dime?" said Aunt Abby. Coco rolled her eyes upward.

"You're wearing the same one, you old bat," Mrs. Carter spat.

"But it looks good on me," Aunt Abby retorted.

"I hate to admit it, but it does. It suits your heart-shaped face." Mrs. Carter inched closer to Aunt Abby and adjusted her hat down a little.

"All right, I'll concede it suits you as well."

"Aren't you glad I talked us into buying it?"

Aunt Abby nodded. "Why don't you pour us a brandy to toast your sage decision?"

"I can get on board with that." Pushing off the couch, Mrs. Carter made her way to the bar of Coco's Malibu home.

Shaking her head, Coco pushed off the sofa and made her way to her bedroom. Closing the door, she turned on the television and sat back to watch her affair unfold on several stations. Coco broke into a big grin when the photographs of her and Alex locking lips flashed on the screen. She wondered how Carlo was going to like them.

IT WAS NOON AND STEVE WAS at The Burger Shack, across from the construction site. The noise in the place was dense and tangible. Kenny Rogers' whiskey-soaked voice floating from the jukebox was barely audible. The air was ripe with the smell of grilled meat and fried foods.

Steve sat at his usual spot at the bar and had his daily fill of a double cheeseburger, fries, and beer. Taking a bite of his burger, Steve chased it with beer. There is nothing like a good grilled burger to replenish a man's energy after a morning of hard manual labour.

Reaching for the ketchup bottle, Steve paused when he caught a glimpse of Coco's face flashing on the television propped on the corner shelf. His eyes cemented to the screen. Steve saw the photos of Coco in a white thong bikini that left little to the imagination. Her arms were chained around the man's neck, and her lips locked with his in a passionate kiss. The photographs were long shots and grainy, but Steve could make out the man wasn't Carlo.

Dropping the hamburger on his plate, Steve signalled for Jason behind the counter to raise the volume on the television. Listening intently to the reporter, he didn't like what he heard. Only months after Coco vowed her love for Carlo, she had moved on to a new, younger love interest.

In a fluorescent Speedo, the man looked tall, muscular, and rich. The yacht sailing over blue waters off the coast of Monaco they were photographed on was worth millions. Steve looked down at his dirty fingernails, his dusty sweatshirt, and stained jeans.

How was he to compete?

Where you came from stayed with you. You could clean it up, dress it up, but it was always underneath. Steve would always be a construction worker.

He was never getting Coco back.

Steve ordered a double whiskey to wash away the feeling of hopelessness.

Chapter 31

A PANICKED EMMA walked through the door Steve held open. She'd put off the doctor's visit for two months, but Steve laid down the law. She and the baby were his family, he told her, and he wanted both looked after.

Emma had no option but to relent and let Steve drive her to the doctor's appointment he scheduled.

"I want you and our baby to get the best care, Emma." Steve and Emma sat in Dr. Walton's waiting room, waiting to be called.

"I know you do. I'm... scared. You know if...." She left the sentence hanging.

"I know you are, but after what we've gone through, doesn't it make sense we get Dr. Walton to monitor your pregnancy?" He said it with a sweetness and tenderness that amplified her guilt and uneasiness.

Worry scored a deep line between Emma's brows. How was she going to get out of this bind? How was Steve going to react when the doctor told him she wasn't pregnant? That she was never pregnant.

She'd dug herself deep into this hole.

Emma felt the quick jolt of panic, and she pushed to her feet. "I can't be here."

Steve caught her hand, held it tight. "Please, Emma. I'm right here with you can count on me to be through anything that comes."

Emma stared down at her shoes. "I know you will be. I just... I can't do this again, Steve."

"Sit down, Emma, relax. I don't want you stressing yourself out. Please, sit." He patted the seat she'd vacated.

"You don't understand, Steve," she said, looking around the waiting room filled with pregnant women, dreamily stroking their bulging tummies.

The blonde across from her positively glowed. Emma imagined her baby would have the same brilliant blue eyes she had. A few seats over the pretty brunette with straight hair and bangs that rode down to her eyelashes reached for her husband's hand and laid it on her tummy when the baby kicked. Next to her, grandma coaxed her rambunctious two-year-old granddaughter to talk to the baby sister or brother, in her mommy's tummy.

Emma's eyes watered. She'd give her soul to be in those women's shoes.

"Please, don't cry, Emma. It's going to be fine this time. I can feel it in my bones."

"No, it's not going to be fine, Steve." Emma was seconds from confessing when the secretary called out her name.

STABBING THE KEY INTO THE LOCK, Steve slammed the door to their home open. "I doubt Dr. Walton lied when he said you weren't pregnant or have been in the past few weeks."

Emma jumped out of the way when Steve tossed the keys on the console table. "I'm sorry, Steve."

"You've been saying that the whole drive home. What I want to hear is an explanation." His searing eyes burned into her. "I want you to be straight with me."

Silently, she walked past him and headed to the kitchen. Steve followed her and watched her reach into the refrigerator for the bottle of Valpolicella. She poured herself a glass and drank deep.

"How am I supposed to trust you again?" The anger snapped in his voice.

The irony, Emma thought and tossed back a good portion of her wine to keep herself from saying precisely what was on her mind.

"Christ, Emma, say something. Why did you lie to me about being pregnant? Do you know how excited I was when you told me you were ready to try again? And when you told me you were pregnant, I was ecstatic for us. I'd even picked out new names."

That knocked the wind out of Emma, and the tears welled in her eyes. Blinking them back, she remained silent. Nothing she'd say would justify lying to him about being pregnant with the child he wanted as much as she did.

She hadn't been able to give him the child he wanted, and now there was a big lie at the heart of their marriage.

And it was her fault.

There was no coming back from this. Emma ran out of the room with Steve calling after her demanding an explanation.

SILENCE IN THE HOUSE SEEMED THUNDEROUS when Emma stepped out of the bedroom where she'd spent it alone all night. Her eyes were rimmed-red and swollen from crying. Her head drumming in steady rhythm at her temples, Emma went in search of Tylenol.

The door to the second bedroom was wide open, and the bed hadn't been slept in. Emma didn't find Steve splayed on the living room sofa where she figured he'd spent the night. Steve wasn't in the kitchen or the bathroom.

Steve wasn't anywhere in the house.

Struggling with the cold fear of loneliness that descended on her, she felt a new wave of tears springing to her eyes.

Emma had no one but herself to blame.

Chapter 32

SOMETIMES YOU OPEN up a door you think is safe and the flames of hell burn through. This was now her new hell, Emma thought, watching Steve slide into his car and drive away. He knew she was at the window but didn't once bother to glance her way.

He'd moved into the basement apartment and refused to speak to Emma or take her calls.

Emma turned down her mother's invitation to Christmas lunch with the excuse of a cold. There would be too many questions if she showed up alone. How was she to explain the reason Steve wasn't with her? If Emma's mother found out about her lie, what she'd done to Steve, she'd never hear the end of it.

Emma reached into her jeans pocket for the key. Eyeing it for a while, she had a mind to use it. Once or twice, after Steve left for work, Emma was tempted to sneak into the basement apartment. To slide into his bed, snuggle with his pillow, and breathe in his scent was what she wanted to do.

Emma missed him in their bed. Not that Steve was the cuddling type, but his warm, naked body next to her in bed was one of the few pleasures in her life. She missed his scent. She missed the lingering sweetness of his Polo cologne that trailed him after his morning shave. Emma missed Steve.

She wished she could undo the harm she caused, but wishing didn't fix anything.

Her life would be so much simpler if she didn't love Steve as much as she did. Coco was right when she said that a relationship between a man and woman worked best when she didn't cross the line into love. You stood to get your heartbroken when you did.

Emma's eyes followed Steve's car as he reversed it out of the driveway. When the backlights faded in the distance, Emma walked away from the window. She had to get ready for work, or she'd miss her bus.

"HE'S BEEN LIVING IN THE BASEMENT apartment going on two months. I don't know what he's going to do when his parents get back from Florida next month. I guess I'm going to have to tell my mother everything and move back home." Emma set the cheesecake topped with fresh strawberries on the table and cut two triangles. "Homemade." She slid the plate to Mary.

"You've become quite the Betty Crocker." The cake was too tempting to pass up, and she spooned a generous piece. "This is delicious, Emma,"

"It's not so difficult to follow a good recipe."

"Says you. I may be able to name every bone in the body, but I guarantee you I wouldn't know where to start on how to make a cheesecake as good as this, recipe or not." Mary spooned a second and third portion and chased it with black coffee. "Anyway, back to the more important topic. You need to talk to Steve, your husband, not your mother."

"I can't. Besides, I want him to come back to me on his own. I don't want to coerce him into anything."

Mary set her fork down. "Steve needs to know, Emma."

"I know he does, but no, I'm not telling him. Who knows, I'm barely six weeks into this pregnancy. I may have another miscarriage." Emma's eyes watered, and Mary got her a tissue.

"You can't think that way, Emma."

"I wish you were a doctor already, Mary. Maybe you could figure out what's wrong with me."

"I checked Dr. Walton, and he has an excellent reputation. Miscarriages are not uncommon, even for young women. Stay positive for yourself and your baby. So show me a smile." Emma gave Mary a teary grin. "That's better. You know I'm always here for you."

"I know," Emma said, knocking tears out of her eyes.

"I know I've been a bit busy with school and Adam, but you know you can call me anytime."

THREE WEEKS LATER, MARY WAS EMMA's only call when she took the bus from work to the hospital after she felt the trickle of blood down her legs while ringing Mrs. Springsteen's groceries.

Mary was By Emma's side the entire five hours she underwent the necessary tests ordered by Dr. Walton to determine how best to address her bleeding. Mary was the calming element for Emma while they waited for the results.

Mary was the person by Emma's side when Dr. Walton confirmed Emma's worst fears that she'd suffered a miscarriage.

AFTER THE FIRST FEW KNOCKS ON the basement door, Mary blew out a breath. "I know you're in there, Steve. Open up because I'm not going away." Mary launched into another knocking bout when Steve didn't open the door.

"Stop that," Steve said, swinging the door open. Over his left shoulder, a plaid tea towel hung, and his hands were covered with oven mitts.

"You should know better than to think I'd issue empty threats." Mary walked past Steve without waiting for an invitation.

"What do you want, Mary. I'm busy."

The apartment was clouded with the smoke flowing from the open oven door. Bowls, dishes, and cutlery cluttered the small kitchen counter and sink. A charred, smoking chicken sat in the sink under cold running water.

"Are you trying to set the place on fire?" Mary waved smoke from her face.

"I was trying to make that roast chicken Emma makes. You know the one with the baby carrots, potatoes, and tiny onions?"

Mary flicked her eyes toward the sink. "Yeah, that's not it."

"She makes it look so simple. I need to leave the door open for a few minutes to let the smoke clear. It's going to get chilly in here." He cautioned Mary when she started shrugging out of her coat. "If you're here to talk me into getting back with Emma, I don't want to hear it."

"Well, I am, and you're going to listen." Mary watched Steve turn the sink water to full flow to drown her out. "I can be here all day."

He turned the water off and walked to the refrigerator. "Do you want a beer?"

"I'll have a drop of yours in a glass." Mary waited until he joined her on the couch.

"I assume you know what Emma did to me." Nodding, Mary took the half-filled glass of beer he handed her. "And I hope you don't condone her actions."

"I don't and told her so."

"It's inexcusable and unforgivable what she did."

"It is."

"She toys with my emotions, fills me with the hope of becoming a father and then rips my heart out."

"She did that."

"It was poor judgment and an incredible lack of disrespect and disregard for me." He sucked down beer. "Nothing you could say can make up for what she did."

"She found the boxes you stashed in the garage, in the corner, under the blue tarp." Mary watched Steve's hardened dark eyes wane into a look of pure shock. "She reacted. It wasn't the right reaction, but it was one of betrayal, which you set off."

There was a pause, a deep sigh. "Shit."

"Shit, indeed. That," Mary stabbed a stiff finger into his chest, "was poor judgment and an incredible lack of disrespect and disregard for her." She kept her voice calm and even, but her eyes were laser-focused on his. "What would you have done if the roles were reversed? If you'd found boxes chock-full of stuff of a man she actually loved."

That shook him enough to have the flush rising to his cheeks. "You're showing your colour, Steve."

Steve rose, took a few steps along the kitchen tile. "Why didn't she say something?"

Her eyebrows lift in wonder. Men could be so obtuse. "Really, Steve?" He opened his mouth, closed it again. "Thought so. Anyway, that's only partly why I'm here."

He raked his fingers through his hair "Christ, there's more?"

"Emma had another miscarriage."

Steve said nothing for a moment while the next wave of shock filtered through his system. "I don't believe it."

"Believe it. She set out to seduce you to get herself pregnant before you found out she wasn't. And, well, she got pregnant."

"Christ, does she keep anything from you?"

"Friends don't."

"Yeah, okay. How am I to trust her anymore when she's seducing me, lying to me?" He raked fingers through his hair. "Christ, what else has she done?"

"Do you blame her for any of it?"

Steve swiped his hands over his face. "When ... when did she have the miscarriage?"

"Last night. She's in the hospital. She's going in for a D&C procedure this afternoon, and...."

"Is she all right? Why did you leave her alone?" Before Mary could say anything, Steve rushed to the closet and dug his jacket out. "I need to go to her."

"She doesn't want you there." Steve came to attention. "She doesn't know I'm here telling you any of this." It was getting chilly in the apartment, and Mary rose to close the front door.

The fierce urge to protect her was strong in him now, and he said, "I need to go to her."

"You do, but not out of pity or out of a sense of spousal duty. She doesn't want or needs that. If you go to her, it's to be her husband. A proper husband, Steve. To her detriment, she loves you."

Steve gave Mary an arched look. "You've always had a way with words."

"She knows you'll never love her as you do, Coco, but she hoped you'd at least fall into it in time."

"I do love her," he said.

"What you love is the woman who keeps your home, takes care of you, washes your clothes, fulfills your sexual needs, and cooks your food." Mary aimed her eyes toward the kitchen that had stopped smoking. "She needs to be loved as your wife as a woman." He glanced away to avoid her penetrating gaze. "I'm heading to the hospital now if you want to come with me."

"I do. I'll drive."

"Fine with me. Oh, and you're getting rid of those boxes and anything relating to Coco before Emma comes home."

Steve followed Mary out the door, digesting what she asked of him.

Chapter 33

Fall 2002

MARY'S HOT STONE massage would be over in minutes, and Emma decided to wait outside her room for her. Minutes later, when Mary showed up, Emma followed her into her room.

Mary's body glowed under a thin layer of sweat, and her hair was tied into a smooth ponytail. She shrugged out of her U of T sweatshirt, wiped her face with a towel, and turned on the TV. CNN flashed on the screen.

"I think I saw Cate Blanchett and Halle Berry by the pool."

"And?" Mary shrugged it off in a casual dismissive gesture.

Emma sat at the edge of the bed. "They're like top celebrities."

"I repeat, and?"

"Hot stone massage is the best, isn't it?" Emma fell back on her elbows, watched Mary pour herself cucumber water from the decanter on the round table. "I don't know how I'm going to live without them once I leave this place because you know I couldn't possibly afford them."

"Maybe you can talk Coco into giving you free passes." Mary tipped the glass to her lips and drank.

"I couldn't ask her for that."

"I have a feeling she'd have no problem giving you lifetime access to this place." It's the least she could do after what she did to you. "She does own the place."

"That would be nice." Emma watched Mary go through her dresser drawer for her running gear.

"Yes, that's our Coco generous to a fault," Mary said, with a quiet kind of bitterness.

"Are you going for a run?"

"You're not good at small talk, Emma. Just say what you came to say."

"Coco wants us to join her for dinner at her place."

"I don't think so." Mary changed into her sports bra and slipped a mauve hoodie over her head. "The only reason I'm still here is that I promised Adam I'd take in this relaxing—pfft, relaxing—weekend."

"Please, Mary, I told her I'd try to get you there. She says she has something important to tell us."

The flickers of fear snaked up Mary's spine as the flash of memory from her last conversation with Coco when she demanded she disappear struck her. Coco was going to tell Emma everything. Coco hadn't admitted it when Mary confronted her earlier in the day, but she sensed it in her bones it was the reason they were there.

After all these years, Mary didn't think guilt was getting the better of Coco, but here they were.

Coco was going to unravel everything. She was going to implicate Mary right along with her as a means to absolve her soul. Why do it now? Why, after ten years, did Coco suddenly need to do it? If Coco told Emma the raw truth, Emma would be left to deal with an ugly reality.

Mary grieved for the time she'd lost with Emma. She hoped she could make that time up, but she couldn't face Emma, not after what Coco did, what she knew. Mary would not play a part in Coco's scheme, even after she told her that grief and the hammer that had recently fallen changed her, and she was bent on making amends.

Mary was the author of the plan for her and Coco to disappear from Emma's life. As much as Mary had done it for Emma's benefit, she didn't believe Emma would see it that way. There were times Mary doubted she had done it for Emma. Deceiving Emma was easier to deal with than telling her the truth.

"Will you come to dinner, Mary?" Emma looked at Mary with pleading eyes.

"I'm sorry, Emma, I won't join the dinner." She slid her ponytail through the slit of her cap and walked to the night table. "I gotta go. I want to get my run in before sundown." She reached for her sunglasses, cell phone, and earphones.

Emma needed more time to persuade Mary to change her mind. "Can I come with you?" Emma said, unexpectedly.

Mary pulled out her earphones, and Emma heard Jennifer Lope getting loud. "You want to go for a run?"

Emma nodded. "I know I may slow you down, but I've been thinking of taking it up." Her reply caused Mary to lift a brow. "Well, can I?"

"Sure." Mary walked to the dresser, pulled out a neon green turtleneck sweater, black tights, and running vest. "Change into these. Your running shoes aren't meant for running, but they'll have to do. I don't have a spare."

"Do you have a support bra?"

"I only brought the one, but let's get real. You don't need it." The smirk twisted Mary's lips.

BEFORE SETTING OFF ON THEIR RUN, Mary led Emma through her warm-up routine. The late afternoon sun washed down out of a clear sky. The woody aroma of soil, horses, and forest flowed in the air along with the sweet scents from Chef's kitchen.

"You're chilly now, but you'll warm up once we start running." Mary reached for the sunglasses on her head and slipped them on.

Emma followed Mary across the front of the lodge to the side and down the parking lot crowded with Ferrari's, Corvettes, Jaguars and every exotic car imaginable. They veered toward the inconspicuous path, past the Keep Out sign. They ran beyond the shelter of trees shielding Coco's cottage from spa visitors. At the end of the trail, Mary came to an abrupt stop. Thirty seconds later, Emma ran into her.

"Why'd you stop?" Emma pushed the sunglasses back in place. "What's wrong?" she asked when Mary's eyes stayed fixated on the silver Mercedes parked in Coco's driveway.

"That's Adam's car."

Emma's gaze cut to the car. "Are you sure?"

"I think I know my husband's car."

"So, what's he doing here?"

"That's what I'd like to know," she snapped like a crocodile before sprinting toward Coco's house.

Chapter 34

Spring 1982

WHEN EMMA CAME out of the anesthesia, she opened her eyes to Steve looking down at her. She felt the warmth of his large, strong hand enveloping hers.

Not a dream. He was there, by her side.

"Hi." Steve gave her a soft smile. She looked so small, so fragile. "How are you feeling?"

"I've been better." Emma's voice was a whisper.

Steve raised the bedsheet to cover her when she shivered. "I'm sorry I wasn't there for you, Emma." However, calm his voice, his eyes were a storm of emotion at the thought she'd taken the bus to the hospital while bleeding and traumatized by the impending loss.

What kind of husband and man was he to give his wife no recourse but deal with such a horrible experience on her own? An uncaring, pathetic man with a fragile ego, he told himself.

Steve slid a hand around to the back of her neck, propped a second pillow to make her more comfortable. "Better?"

"Yes, thank you."

"I'm sorry, Emma."

She shook her head. "It's me who's sorry for pulling such a stupid stunt. I never meant to hurt you or lie to you."

"It's me who needs to apologize. Mary told me everything. I'm so sorry, Emma. The boxes will be gone. Everything will be gone. I promise" He took her hand, linked his fingers with hers. "I promise. It'll just be you and me from now on," he said the words she'd been waiting to hear for so long, but it was little comfort then. It was going to be just the two of them. She stared at him, and her eyes filled up.

"I don't think I'm able to give you the children you want, Steve. I'd understand if you want to walk away."

He brushed a finger to wipe the tears streaking down her cheeks. "You can't get rid of me that easily. What I want is to get you out of here and home."

"Did you hear what I said, Steve?" She winced when the sharp pain shot through her lower abdomen.

"Don't move. You've just come out of surgery. And yes, I heard you, but none of that matters. I want you out of here and home."

Emma wavered a moment, measuring the man before her. "Really, Steve?"

He touched her lips with his. "Really."

Chapter 35

MARY REMOVED THE lid from the container and set it in Emma's hands. "It's wonton soup, mainly broth. It'll go down easily."

"Thanks. Hot soup is going to hit the spot. Where's Adam?"

"He's catching up on medical reports. I was studying, but I need a break." Mary sat at the kitchen table and reached for her container of soup. At the centre of the table, a glass vase held a dozen pink carnations in clear water. "How's ... everything?"

"If you're asking if Steve's been a good husband, the answer is yes. He's been perfect since coming home from the hospital. Thank you." Emma toasted with the soup container.

"No need for thanks. I had a craving for wonton soup." Mary watched Emma struggle to fish a wonton between two wooden chopsticks from her soup.

"You know what I mean." Emma watched Mary rise from the table and walk to the cutlery drawer.

"I thought I taught you how to use chopsticks." Mary swapped the chopsticks in Emma's hand with a spoon. "You did, but it never stuck, and don't dodge. I know you spoke to Steve and whatever you said turned him into a super husband."

"You always said I had a way with words. Where is he, by the way?"

"Working. He encouraged me to take the month off to recuperate and has taken extra shifts to compensate for the income loss." The glowing flush on Emma's face warmed Mary.

Emma looked healthy and happy. She'd had too much heartache and disappointment. It was damn time Steve took care of her and infused some joy in her life. If anyone deserved happiness, it was sweet, kindhearted Emma.

"It's nice to see you happy, Emma."

Emma's smile spread slowly. "I am happy. Steve's been a model husband since I came home from the hospital. He's been attentive and loving. He won't let me lift a finger around the house."

Steve had better keep it up, or he'd have her to deal with. "Good to hear," she said while turning her gaze to the television on the kitchen counter when Coco's voice flowed from it.

The trailer for The Mistress of Covington played on the screen. Emma and Mary watched Coco looking classy and beautiful in a silver, sequin flapper dress with a tassel fringe. Carlo's lips skimmed along her neck as he courted her with wanton words in an attempt to seduce her from her duplicitous husband. When it was over, like a sinful pleasure, it left you wanting more.

"Her movie is releasing in a few months, and if the trailer is any indication, it's going to be a big hit."

"Looks like. Between you and me, I never thought she'd be as good as she is." Mary fished the last wonton from her soup.

"I think Carlo brings out the best in her. I hope they're able to patch up their marriage after her infidelity." Emma rose to put on the coffee.

"Sit back down. I'll do that."

"I need to do more than sit." Emma filled the coffee pot with water. "Coco's affair with Carlo's assistant is still front and center in the tabloids."

"Well, Carlo better get used to it because it won't be her last. If I know Coco, she's relishing the attention she's getting—good or bad. Who'd have thought we'd know a soon-to-be movie star."

"I know, eh?" Emma switched the coffee machine on and collected mugs and sugar, and walked them to the table. "Will you go to see Coco's movie?"

Why should she support the backstabbing bitch who was too important to pick up pen and paper or the telephone to keep in touch with her lowly friends? "I haven't decided."

Emma left it there. Mary was the queen of grudge-holders, and the one she had against Coco was strong in her. "I want to ask you a favour, Mary."

Mary swept her gaze to Emma's face. "What is it? Do you have anything sweet to go with the coffee?"

"There's a banana cake in the fridge and vanilla ice cream in the freezer."

"That'll do." Mary got to her feet and got busy getting dishes, spoons, and a knife. "Well, spill. What's the favour?"

"I want you to help me find out why I've had so many miscarriages. The doctor keeps telling me the miscarriages are stress-related. That a viable pregnancy will happen when it happens, but I know there's something else going on. There's something wrong with me, and I need to know what."

Mary dropped the knife on the cake with a thud. "I'm only in my third year of school, Emma. I don't know that I can be of munchies help to you."

"Isn't U of T like a learning school?"

"Teaching school," Mary corrected.

"Yeah, that. You're smart, Mary. I can be your first patient."

Mary bit back a sigh. "But I don't know what good I'd be to you. You need a fertility specialist or an OB/GYN who specializes in infertility."

"Jesus, you think I'm infertile."

Mary imagined this was how dealing with patients was like, and she said, "It's a term, Emma," with patience and empathy to smooth her out. "Are you sure you want to do this now? You're still processing your recent … experience. And what does Steve say?"

"We haven't discussed it in depth yet, you know how brittle men are when it comes to women's issues, but I don't think he wants to go through the emotional upheaval and stress of another miscarriage."

Mary set the plates with cake and ice cream on the table. "If that's the case, why not hold off for a while. Enjoy your time together with your super husband. You need to focus on you and Steve right now."

"Maybe you're right," Emma said.

There was so much innocent hope and vulnerability in the pleading eyes that stared at Mary it drove her to make the promise she knew she wouldn't be able to keep. "I'll see what I can do."

Chapter 36

THE SCENE WAS everything of the movie premieres Coco had seen on television when she was a kid. Stretch limousines were lined up for blocks. Huge, bright, floodlights, like beacons in the night, reached high into the night sky. Gawking fans kept behind the cordoned barrier shouted for Coco and Carlo's attention when they stepped out of the limousine onto the red carpet in front of Grauman's Chinese Theatre. Some asked for selfies. Others wanted autographs.

Coco wore a Lagerfeld mulberry off the shoulder, floor-length chiffon with a flowing skirt. Her hair tumbled in waves around her face down to her shoulders. Arm linked through Carlo's, with a graceful sway of her hips, she made her way up the red carpet while flashing her practiced smile when the flashes went off.

The shouting fans, the clicking cameras, the millions of eyes around the country fixed on the television watching her every move was intoxicating.

Along the way, she and Carlo stopped to give interviews to anyone flashing a microphone. Coco could do it all day long.

Inside the theatre, Coco mingled with grace and the sophistication of a seasoned celebrity. Whenever the camera panned to Coco, she reacted with the Queenly subtle wave or tipped her champagne glass in salute the way Carlo taught her. At times, she tossed her head back with the pasted smile Carlo told her to do to excess for the cameras. On cue, Coco would peck Carlo on the cheek or lean into him in the affectionate way her fans expected of the fairy tale Hollywood couple. Carlo followed Coco's lead and reciprocated in kind.

The premiere of *The Mistress of Covington* received rave reviews. Coco earned well-deserved acclaim for her screen work. The critics compared her to Audrey Hepburn, Sally Field, and Susan Sarandon. One critic went as far as to label Coco the sweetheart of the silver screen. From that moment, Coco's face and her name became the talk of Hollywood, and her face was splashed across every magazine cover and newspaper in the nation.

The Mistress of Covington set box office records opening weekend, and that was just the beginning.

AT SEPARATE THEATERS, MARY AND EMMA took in Coco's movie. With pride and awe, they watched their friend shine through her talent. They watched Coco perform in a drama with an accent unfamiliar to her, which Mary and Emma knew was out of her comfort zone. Yet, her performance was seamless, flawless. It was Oscar-worthy.

Emma and Mary's lips stretched out in a smile for the friend who'd once been a part of their lives.

"Congratulations, Coco. You've done it." Emma murmured, watching Coco's name scroll below Carlo's on the screen.

"I hate that you're a disloyal bitch to Emma and me, but I'm proud of you, Coco," Mary muttered to herself in the crowded theatre as, with pride, she watched Coco's name flash on the screen. "The world will soon know Coco D'Onofrio."

IN THE FOUR YEARS THAT FOLLOWED, the world came to know and adore Coco D'Onofrio.

Following the launch of *The Mistress of Covington*, scripts and the offers to sign Coco on for obscene amounts of money rolled in. Every director wanted to cast her, and every agent wanted to represent her.

It wasn't long before Coco's name became synonymous with every top movie in Hollywood. To Coco's surprise, she surpassed Carlo's popularity and commanded top billing.

In four years, she put out eight five-star rated movies ranging from drama to comedy. When you thought she'd topped herself, the film that followed elevated her acting skills. Her versatility and range as an actor had her embracing roles she never thought possible. Each time she put out a performance, it left her audience awed.

Coco's movies sold out. She filled theatres, tills, and investors' pockets.

Coco's most remarkable work, and the one she prided, was in *Mary Queen of Scots,* the historical biopic written and directed by Carlo. That performance got Carlo a BAFTA for best director and Coco for best actor, making her the youngest recipient in the award's history.

Chapter 37

MARY'S EYES WERE beyond joyful as she accepted her diploma and waved it in the air in triumph. The speech that followed was articulate, insightful, and memorable. It was Mary through and through. Emma didn't expect any less from the valedictorian of the class of 1987.

Recruited by Mount Sinai Hospital, one week after graduating, Mary began her internship—no time like the present. Alongside Adam, who was on his way to becoming a top-notch oncologist, Mary was getting that much closer to achieving her dream of becoming an OB/GYN. Now, however, Mary leaned toward specializing in infertility.

For four years, Mary saw Emma's struggle to have what many women took for granted. Mary watched her undergo the tests, the prodding of her body in the most intimate nature. After it all, Mary watched Emma suffer through her fourth miscarriage to then be told she'd never have children. For the first time, Mary felt the pain and demand of womanhood and committed to helping women. Seeing Emma and Steve endure heartache and misery for so long gave Mary a new perspective and direction. It steered her to her decision to specialize in infertility.

Mary knew she wouldn't perform miracles but hoped to help women in Emma's circumstances to find answers sooner. Her goal was to find medical answers for couples to avoid the pain and misery infertility visited in their lives through no choice of their own.

"You knocked it out of the ballpark with that speech, Mary." Emma took her friend into a sisterly hug. "I'm so proud of my brainy friend." She reached for the diploma in Mary's hand, rolled it open to admire.

"Ditto, my valedictorian wonder." Adam kissed Mary, then flicked eyes to the diploma and admired it along with Emma.

"I, for one, want to be the first to address you as Dr. Mary Carter." Steve pecked Mary on the cheek.

"Dr. Mary Carter," Mary murmured. "God, I do like the sound of that."

The chatter of excited students and parents proudly flashing diplomas along with birds flitting through the air, chirping in song under a brilliantly blue sky crowded the air. Professors worked their way through the crowds, meeting the parents and family of the children they'd entrusted to them to shape their future.

"Are you ready to bite the bullet, my soon-to-be husband?" Mary shed her graduation gown and cap to reveal a white, very short, V-neck dress.

Her chestnut hair hung loosely over her shoulders. Her face was lightly touched with makeup, and her lips glossy pink—a rarity for Mary. Adam thought it suited her just fine.

"I am if you promise to look this good every day of our married life." Adam played his mouth over hers.

"I'd say get a room, but there's one waiting for you in Cuba where you'll be honeymooning for one week after you tie the knot today. It's our wedding gift to you," Steve said.

Mary glanced over to Steve and Emma with a surprised look. "Thank you, but you didn't have to do that."

"We did. It's a thank you for all your help these past years." Emma's eyes stung, and Steve interjected.

"You helped us get answers, Mary, and we're grateful for that. So take your present and enjoy it."

"We will. Thank you." Mary leaned in to give Emma and Steve a hug, and Adam followed.

"On that note, we better get moving. We're supposed to be at city hall in front of the justice of the peace in forty minutes." Adam slung an arm around Mary's shoulder.

Anticipating Mary, Emma said, "Your bouquet is in the car, and I booked *Carmelina's Ristorante* for dinner. They're expecting twenty of us. And yes, there are boutonnieres for Adam, your best man," Emma rolled her eyes toward Steve, "and your dad. Have I fulfilled my matron of honour duties?"

"Just checking."

Emma arched dark brows. "Sure, you were."

"Adam, let's you and I round up the troops and get everyone heading to city hall," Steve suggested.

"Right behind you." Adam led Steve through the crowd to find his parents, Mary's and Emma's and their four high-spirited children.

Thoughts of Coco swam into Emma. She was missing so much of their life. Glancing at the faces around them, Emma thought that Coco should be amongst them.

"You wish Coco were here," Mary said when she saw Emma go thoughtful.

"No, I was thinking how nicely Steve and Adam get on. It's nice to see."

"It's me, Emma, don't lie."

"All right. I do wish she were here celebrating this momentous moment with us. You've just become a doctor, Mary. If I recall, it was Coco who encouraged you to pursue medicine. She always told you that except for your judgy bedside manner, I'm quoting Coco, you'd make a great doctor."

The smirk twisted Mary's lips. "I'll give her that one, but she wouldn't be here even if we'd invited her. She's too busy working on her next movie," and selfishness.

"Maybe, but we didn't even try."

Because she hasn't answered any of the letters I sent her, and I'm done chasing after her. Mary's head shot up, her eyes alive with anger. "Believe me when I tell you, Emma, Coco wouldn't set aside her very important life to be here for a simple graduation."

"Maybe, but she might have come if she knew today was also your wedding day."

Doubt it. "Well, it's too late now."

"Steve and I have put in the adoption papers," Emma said, to change the topic.

Temper waned into an interested gaze. "That's great, Emma. I'm happy for you."

"We're hoping to get a baby or a toddler before the end of the year."

"That's great news." Mary tipped her head to look at Emma. "Why am I sensing you're not as happy as you should be?"

"I think Steve's doing this for me. I don't think he wants someone else's child. To compromise, I've agreed to foster before we adopt."

"It's a reasonable concession. He'll change his mind once the child becomes a part of your family."

"I hope so."

"He will. Men are like puppies. They need time to adjust to the newness in their life."

"Steve's right. You do have a way with words."

"Can't deny that." Mary caught sight of Adam and Steve and the procession of people they brought with them. "Now, let's get me married."

Chapter 38

CHARLOTTE WAS HER name, and Emma fell in love with her the minute they set her in her arms. She was two days old with dark, intelligent eyes. Her hair was silky soft. Her tiny heart-shaped face was the most beautiful thing Emma had ever seen.

"I'm your mommy." Emma drew in the baby's scent and embraced how perfect she felt in her arms. "She's going to be a pianist." Emma held out Charlotte's tiny hand for Steve to see her long fingers.

"Let's not get ahead of ourselves," he said glibly.

Men are like puppies. They need time to adjust to the newness in their life. With Mary's words in mind, Emma set the baby in Steve's arms. "She wants to be held by her daddy." The baby curled and lay in the circle of Steve's arms, and her sleepy eyes focused on Steve's face. "She's looking at you, Steve."

A frown creased Steve's brow, and he started to hand the baby back to Emma. He paused, sighed when Charlotte reached up with her tiny hand to stroke his stubbled face and left her hand there. Relaxing into a smile, he stared at her for a long moment.

The power of a child's touch could entrance a grown man, Emma thought. "She likes you. Talk to her." He opened his mouth, then closed it again. "Go on, let her hear your voice." She encouraged.

"Hi, I'm your daddy, at least temporarily." He stroked the baby's cheek with his fingertip. "You're a sweet girl, Charlie." Steve tilted his gaze from the baby to Emma. "Can we call her Charlie?"

"I like it."

"Mommy's okay with us calling you Charlie. So, Charlie Jenkins, it will be." With the greatest of caution, Steve set the baby in her chair and lifted it by the handle. "Let's take our daughter home," he said, with a tenderness that filled Emma with pure love. Never had she felt such love.

"All right, Steve, whatever you say."

ALONG WITH THE JOY AND LAUGHTER that filled Emma and Steve's home, there was excited terror. They were parents, responsible for a tiny human being dependent on them for her very existence, but they were up for the challenge. The love they had for this baby went beyond the realm of imagination. They would do anything for their daughter.

Emma and Steve's home and marriage weren't broken anymore. Steve's mind wasn't full of Coco. It was full of his daughter and wife. Steve and Emma were closer than they'd ever been. Charlie had strengthened their bond and cemented them as a couple.

Emma felt so happy, so full of hope, so full of love.

Arched at Charlie's bedroom door, Emma watched Steve rock Charlie to sleep in his arms. There had been nights when Emma found him sitting in the rocking chair he built and set across Charlie's crib watching her sleep. I wanted to make sure she's okay, he'd say and remained watching her for hours.

Emma cleared her throat to get his attention. "Dinner's on the table."

"I'm coming." He stood and ever so gently lay Charlie in her crib.

Watching her big, strong husband morph into a gentle teddy bear made Emma's heart swell with joy. "Isn't it a bit too warm in here?" she said, of the room, transformed into a nursery.

Lace curtains, stamped with unicorns, framed the window. Walls washed in pastel pink were covered in framed pictures of Charlie. Gone was the popcorn ceiling. In its place, there was a mural of fluffy white clouds and stars for Charlie to wake up to.

"She likes it that way." He brought the cover over Charlie's back.

"She told you this?"

He shook his head. "A daddy knows his daughter."

Emma exchanged a contemplative look with Steve. "You're happy?"

"Very much so." He walked to Emma and glided his lips over hers. "And I'm also famished. What's for dinner?"

ALTHOUGH THEIR BLOOD DIDN'T COURSE THROUGH Charlie, the love that existed in Emma and Steve, for that little girl was as strong as honed steel. She was their daughter.

They had nursed her through her first fever. They stayed by her crib during her teething and her bout of colic. They coached her to take her first step and celebrated with her when she did. They were by her side when she said her first word—dada—and applauded her accomplishment.

On the anniversary of their second year of fostering, Emma and Steve put in their papers to adopt Charlie. The social worker said their record was stellar and ticked all the boxes for adoption. She assured them their chance for adoption was very good. Charlie's mother, a scared sixteen-year-old who gave her up the moment she birthed her, hadn't expressed an interest in her daughter's life.

That is until the adoption papers were days from being finalized and Charlie's mother refused to sign them. Whatever her reason, she demanded Charlie's return.

To say that Steve and Emma were brokenhearted was an understatement. Charlie was their daughter, and no one could tell them otherwise. She was a part of them, of their family. She had been since she was two days old. Turning their daughter over to the woman who'd given her flesh and blood up seconds after giving birth was the hardest thing Emma and Steve had to do.

That moment marked a change in their relationship.

The heartbreak on top of the hurt, the shock of losing her daughter, sent Emma straight into depression. Her home and marriage were broken—again. This time, however, drained of all hope, Emma didn't care what became of her and Steve.

Chapter 39

UNDER THE COVER of night, in the remote airport north of Toronto, Coco, Carlo, Alex, and Fredo alit the private jet leased under Jane Smith—Coco's birth name. The last thing they wanted was to attract attention or have the press and paparazzi on their trail.

Walking across the tarmac, the whisper of a summer night breeze carried the smell of jet fuel. Above, the moon was luminous in a black sky dotted with stars. Fog smoked along the ground, floated through the trees and shadows of the night. Beyond the tarmac, the lights of the city spread out like luminous fireflies in the dark. It felt like a scene from a movie set, but it wasn't.

Coco had come home.

Loading the luggage into the taxi, Alex gave the driver the address to Aunt Abby's home. Aunt Abby's house was the perfect hideaway. No one would track Carlo there or suspect he'd taken up residency in the quaint redbrick home on Weston Road when Aunt Abby, with Mrs. Carter, lived in his.

Together the two women were formidable and could drive away any reporters that crossed their path. Coco was counting on it. Kept in the dark for long enough, the media and their gossip consuming audiences would soon enough move on to the next story.

Coco felt a mixture of excitement and fear when she placed the call to Mary's childhood home in the morning.

After her years of absence, she'd understand if Mary wanted nothing to do with her, but Coco hoped she'd take her call. She needed Mary's help, now more than ever.

Mary's mother informed Coco her daughter was married and no longer lived there. In the pit of Coco's stomach, a knot tightened. Coco wondered how much she'd missed of Mary's life.

Regaining her composure, Coco dialled the number Mary's mother gave her for Mount Sinai. It took a ten-minute hold to get through to Mary at the Mount Sinai Fertility Clinic.

"Dr. Mary Carter." Mary's voice was confident and authoritative. Coco's lungs hitched, and her throat seemed to close up. For a moment, she remained soundless. "Dr. Mary Carter, how can I help you?" Mary repeated.

Mary was about to hang up when Coco managed to say, "Hi, Mary, it's Coco."

In the ensuing silence, Coco could hear the cacophony of sounds of clinic life. Telephones shrilled with incoming calls. The receptionist directed patients to examining rooms, the high-pitched tone of a fax machine droned.

"Please don't hang up, Mary," Coco pleaded when she sensed Mary was about to do so.

"I'm here." Her voice was stern and cold. "To what do I owe the exalted pleasure of the great Coco D'Onofrio taking the time to call me?" In true Mary fashion, she used the name as an insult, not flattery.

Coco brushed the deserved jab aside. "I need your help, Mary."

"Of course you do. It's so typical of you to come around only when you need something. This won't take long, Debbie. I'll be there in a moment." Mary called out when the nurse informed her Mrs. Shade was waiting in room 5. "I'm swamped, Coco. I don't have time for you."

"I'm not calling for me, Mary. I'm calling for Carlo. He needs your help." The despair in Coco's voice broke through Mary's hardened posturing.

"Debbie, I'm going to be a few more minutes. Can you take Mrs. Shade's blood pressure and get her blood work started?" Mary conveyed additional incoherent instructions with authority before she turned her attention back to the telephone. "What's the problem, Coco?"

Noting Mary's anger filtered out of her voice Coco ventured to make her request. "I can't do it over the phone. Can you come to Aunt Abby's after work? I know I'm asking for a lot."

"You think?"

"Please, Mary, and bring your medical bag."

MARY TOOK A CALMING BREATH BEFORE she knocked on the back door as Coco instructed her to do.

Coco opened the door. For a long moment, she stared at Mary. The person before her wasn't the girl she left behind. Mary was a woman, a professional woman.

Her hair, now a tawny shade of brown, fountained down her face to her shoulders. She didn't have an ounce of makeup on her face but needed none. She wore a tapered Armani jacket against a flowing silk blouse and a pencil skirt. The ballerinas at her feet were fashionably comfortable. Comfort over fashion was Mary's credo. In her right hand, she held a medical bag and looked every bit the doctor she was.

"Thank you for coming, Mary," Coco said because she couldn't think of anything else to say.

"I know it's late, but I came as soon as I could. It was a busy day at the clinic."

"No. No, I, ah, appreciate you fitting us in." Coco was tongue-tied. A first, Mary thought of her celebrity friend, who never failed to have a word when the microphones were pointed at her.

Coco's hair was tied into a messy ponytail. Her eyelashes weren't mascaraed, her face was unpainted, and her eyes looked tired. She wore a red and white striped T-shirt and faded jeans, and still, she looked every bit the beautiful luminary Mary had seen on the screen.

"Are you going to invite me in?" Mary said, after a floating silence.

"Yes, of course, I'm sorry. Please come in." Coco stepped aside, and Mary walked into the kitchen. The smell of brewing coffee and stuffy heat came at her. "Would you like a cup of coffee or a cold drink?"

"Coffee's good, thank you."

"You still take it black?"

"I do," Mary said as Fredo trotted into the kitchen and propped himself on his rump. "Hello, and who are you?"

"That's Fredo. Say hello, Fredo," Coco said.

Mary's lips curled in an amused smile when Fredo offered her a canine grin along with his paw. "You're a smart one." Mary reached down for Fredo's paw and gave him a well-deserved head scratch.

Coco had to smile when Mary reached into her bag for a disinfecting wipe to sanitize her hand. It was so much like Mary to do so.

"This is Alex," Coco said when he walked into the kitchen. "This is Mary Carter. She's the doctor I'm hoping will help us."

Mary took the offered hand from the man she recognized as Coco's lover from the scandalous affair.

"We very much appreciate you coming, Dr. Carter. I'll take her to Carlo," Alex said to Coco when he released her hand.

"All right. I'll be in shortly." Coco set four mugs on the counter as Alex escorted Mary to the living room.

"Carlo, this is Dr. Carter, Coco's friend." Alex dimmed the volume on the television news.

Mary took stock of the man who had no resemblance to the bigger-than-life star she'd seen on the screen. He had sallow skin and sunken cheeks. His eyes were tinged yellow, and his physical reaction was slow. Although the house was warm, a plaid throw covered his legs. Carlo looked twenty pounds thinner than he had on the screen. Mary doubted it was due to the camera adding pounds on you.

The handsome looking man who radiated sexual energy on the screen looked frail and small against the sofa's cushions.

"It's nice to meet you, Dr. Carter." Carlo flashed his trademark suave smile and offered Mary his feeble hand.

"He has AIDS," Alex said when Mary started to reach for his hand.

If the sudden shock of Alex's revelation surprised Mary, it didn't register on her face. She met Carlo's hand and pumped it. "It's a pleasure to meet you, Mr. D'Onofrio."

"It's Carlo. As my doctor, you're far more important than I am. You are my doctor, aren't you?" Carlo's eyes calm and level on hers, he waited for her response.

She clasped his hand between hers with a warm smile. "I am, and it's Mary."

Carlo's eyes brightened. "Thank you, Mary. If you're as good a doctor as you are pretty, I have nothing to worry about." Carlo's voice was a hoarse whisper.

"I don't know about that, but I can assure you I always try my very best."

Arched in the doorway, the cup of coffee in her hand, Coco watched the scene between Mary and Carlo. She blinked the moisture from her eyes. "Coffee's on."

"Did you hear that, Coco? She's agreed to be my doctor."

"I did, honey. Have this while Alex and I talk to Mary." Coco set the four pills in Carlo's shaking hand and the cup of coffee in the other. She waited until he took his pills before dragging a spread over his fragile shoulders. "Fredo will keep you company. Won't you, baby." Coco bent down to kiss the dog. As much as Mary cringed at the microbial exchange between dog and human, Coco's loving gesture surprised her.

"Thank you, Mary, for being so kind and respectful not because of who he is or because of his illness, but because it's what he deserves," Coco said when they walked into the kitchen. There were three cups, sugar, cream, and a pot with steaming coffee on a heat plate on the table. Coco gestured for Mary to take a seat.

"His old doctor treated Carlo, the man, not the celebrity. He used to say, 'In this office, you're a patient, nothing more, Carlo and will do what I say. Take your goddamn medication and keep out of the sun when you do.'" Alex scraped the chair back for Mary.

"Dr. Murphy died unexpectedly of a heart attack a month ago," Coco added. "He was the only doctor we trusted to take care of Carlo."

"Well, I'm happy to help, but I'm an OB/GYN specializing in infertility. I'll give Carlo a checkup now that I'm here, but he's going to need...."

"You, Dr. Carter." There was genuine desperation in Alex's voice.

Coco laid a gentle hand on Alex's shoulder. "We need you, Mary." Coco set a plate of ham and cheese sandwiches and a garden salad in front of Mary. "It's my specialty. I figured you'd be hungry since you came straight from work."

"Thank you, I am." Mary forked salad. "That's surprisingly good."

"It's the Italian dressing." Alex held up the dressing bottle. The label bore Carlo's face, and below it read Carlo D'Onofrio's Original. "It's Carlo's mom's recipe. One of Carlo's many business ventures. Coco's only specialty is in the way she pours and tosses."

Mary's brow shot up. "Yeah, I didn't think you'd honed in on your domestic side."

"Pfft, as if. The most domestic she gets is making coffee," Alex's disclosure got him a playful elbow plowed into his side, and what Mary deduced was a ploy by Coco to calm him had worked.

Coco tilted her eyes to Mary. "The reason we need you, Mary, is because we don't want Carlo's... situation getting out for public consumption. If it does, it will destroy his legacy, and he'll forever be known as the man who was in the closet all his life and died of AIDS." The emotions pouring out of Coco were real and honest.

"Carlo's worked too hard, given so much of himself to have everything taken from him. To have his legacy destroyed because of people's insecurity and fears of something they don't understand. I, we," Coco reached for Alex's hand, "Won't let that happen. It's why we need you, Mary. We need Carlo looked after by someone we can trust, and that's you. Like Dr. Murphy, I know you'd never sell Carlo out for profit."

Alex rose. "I'll get us a glass of cognac. Can I pour you one, Dr. Carter?"

"It's Mary, and this will do me." Mary took a swig of the coffee in her hand.

"I know you must be livid with me, and I admit I haven't been a friend to you or Emma," Coco took the chair Alex vacated, "But there were secrets I wasn't ready to share. I knew if I spoke to you...."

"I'd be judgmental." Mary watched Alex hand Coco one of the cognac glasses and took the seat next to her.

"I was going to say that I'd let out the secret I promised Carlo and Alex to keep. You know I was never good at keeping secrets from you." Coco looked over at Alex for his consent.

"It's why I got you the drink, liquid courage. Go on." Alex said.

"Christ, I don't know where to start." Coco's gaze stayed focused on the hands wrapped around her mug.

"Let me, Coco," said Alex. "Carlo was diagnosed with HIV the year before he and Coco were married. When he was, the need to take on a wife became more urgent. His mother and I had been pushing Carlo to take on a wife for years to stop the abounding rumours he was gay from circulating and destroying his career. With his diagnoses, stopping the rumours now took priority. In Hollywood, a molehill becomes a mountain in minutes. That's when I set out to find Carlo, the right wife."

"And that was me." Coco jumped in. "I was open-minded, ambitious, and would do anything to get my career into gear. The deal was that I'd pose as his wife, and he'd get my career rolling. I was good with that."

Alex covered Coco's hand and gave it an affectionate squeeze. "And we were grateful to Coco. With her in the picture, not only did the rumour Carlo was gay die out, but she complimented his career. He got the chance to write and direct, a dream of his. Because of Coco, he went on to succeed at it. He was also able to continue his philanthropic work. Giving starving talent a leg up to better their life is something near and dear to him."

"Only Alex, Aunt Abby, me, and of course Carlo were in on this." Coco watched Mary give her a quick, appraising look. "You're thinking this whole scheme is very me."

Mary shook her head. "I'm thinking it's not you at all. Your selflessness is inspiring."

Coco hooted a laugh. "Always direct and to the point. Don't ever change, Mary."

"We know Carlo doesn't have long. Dr. Murphy said he had six months to one year. He's bearing up under the strain of his illness, but…." Alex took a moment to collect himself when he heard the tears in his voice. "We'd like to make his last days as dignified and comfortable as possible. Will you help us, Mary?"

"I will." Mary didn't hesitate. "But I'd like to bring Adam, my husband, into this. He's an oncologist and more experienced with the type of medicinal cocktail Carlo needs. He'll keep your confidence," Mary assured.

"Whatever you think is best. Thank you, Mary," Coco said humbly.

"Yes, thank you, Mary. We're very grateful to you." Alex got to his feet. "If you'll excuse me, I need to check on Carlo."

Mary's eyes followed Alex out of the room. "He seems like a sweet man."

Coco picked up her cognac, drank. "The sweetest."

"The affair between you and him was a PR stunt."

Coco nodded. "Alex is as gay as they come. He and Carlo were together way before they brought me into the picture." Coco walked to the counter and reached into the cookie jar. She pulled out a pack of cigarettes.

"No, that's not going to happen, especially when Carlo's in this house."

Grudgingly, Coco returned them to the cookie jar and set the lid back on. "So, you married a doctor. You achieved everything you set out to do."

"So did you." Mary watched Coco reach for the bottle of cognac on the counter and walk it back to the table.

"I sacrificed relationships, the chance for a family, and friends to pursue my interests and passions." Coco poured herself another drink, sent it streaming down her throat. "But what's done is done. Right now, Carlo is my focus. He's my pretend-husband, but my love for him is real. If he weren't gay, I would have been a real wife to him." She crossed to the window, scanned the colourful backyard garden Aunt Abby's pride and joy.

Roses were just sprouting to life while tulips, impatiens, asters, and purple lupines were in full show. The bleeding hearts Coco had planted with her bare hands dangled bright and pink from green branches.

Coco swivelled to cast her eyes at Mary. "Life's funny. The stronger the feeling you can't have someone, the more you want them." Her smile seemed to be full of both sadness and love, and Mary couldn't help but feel compassion for the broken, lost woman before her.

"When was the last time you had a good night's sleep?"

Coco rubbed at her tired eyes. "What's sleep?"

Mary reached into her medical bag and pulled out a couple of sedatives. "Take one now. It'll help you get a good night's rest."

"I can't. I need to stay with Carlo."

"I'll stay with him. You and Alex need to rest. You both look exhausted, and you're no good to Carlo if you can't function. Doctor's orders."

Miracles could happen, Coco thought, and with Mary, it would for Carlo. It would!

Chapter 40

MARY WAS SEARCHING for the coffee grounds when Coco, in a flowing pink kimono, breezed into the kitchen bright with morning sunshine. She looked relaxed and refreshed.

"Looks as if you got a good night's rest?" Mary reached into the refrigerator for the milk.

"Those pills you gave me knocked me right out." Coco crossed to the coffee machine and found it filled with stale coffee. "I haven't had such a good night's sleep in a long while." She picked up the pot and dumped it in the sink.

"Good." Mary poured milk into a glass and handed it to Coco. "Sit and drink that. It's good for you."

Coco thought better than to argue and took the glass. "Okay, thanks. Coffee would be good too, though."

"I was about to make some. Point me to the coffee."

"In the shelf above the coffee machine."

"You seem to have the essentials, but you're going to need a proper food run." Mary reached for the coffee tin.

"Yeah, Aunt Abby had Bob's Supermarket deliver just the necessities. I'll go out later to properly stock up. How did Carlo sleep?"

"He got a few hours of sleep." Mary poured water into the coffee maker's reservoir and filled the filter with coffee. "Adam and Alex are with him now. Adam is assessing his scripts. He'll make the necessary adjustments to ensure Carlo's comfort." Mary flipped the ON button on the coffee machine and turned to butter the bread that popped from the toaster. "My specialty," she said, setting the toast in front of Coco. "Eat. You need to keep your energy up."

Coco picked up a triangle of toast, nibbled it. "I don't know how to thank you, Mary."

"I'm doing this for Carlo. He needs help, and I swore an oath to help those in medical need. You don't deserve my help." Mary sat, crossed one slender leg over another. She'd shed Armani for tights and a polo shirt. For someone who'd stayed up all night watching over Carlo, she looked wide-eyed and rested.

"You're right, I don't, but as you said, Carlo does, and I thank you. I hate seeing him so fragile, so sick." Tangles of emotions passed across Coco's face. "It's not fair. He's young, has given so much. He still has so much to offer. He's one of the good guys."

It was a thought that crossed Mary all too often when dealing with patients with no recourse. "No, it's not fair, but we need to focus on the now and what we need to do now is to give him the best quality of life we can."

"Yes. Yes, of course."

The coffee machine spurted the last drops into the pot, and Mary got to her feet. "Coffee's ready."

"I'll stick with the milk."

"How did you know I became a doctor?" Mary got straight to the point.

"I didn't know. I suspected it. I know that once you set your mind, you latch on and don't let go."

Mary sat back at the table with a steaming coffee cup in her hands. "You haven't once asked me about Emma?"

Coco lowered her eyes to the white liquid in her glass. "How is Emma?"

"Not well," Mary told Coco of Emma's miscarriages, the adoption, and the eventual loss of the girl. "It broke Emma, and she's plunged into a deep depression. It's destroying her marriage, her."

Coco looked horrified and sad. "Jesus, I didn't know."

"You may have kept abreast of our goings-and-comings if you'd called or answered any of the letters I sent you. Did you even read them?"

Shaking her head, Emma lowered her gaze to her knitted hands. "I couldn't keep in touch."

"I can't wait to hear this excuse."

Coco's gaze stayed focused on her hands as she wound her wedding ring on her finger. "Steve asked me to marry him. I left the ring on the night table, and without as much as a goodbye, I snuck out in the morning while he slept. I went home, packed up my things and left for New York. I knew he'd be looking for me, and Emma kept on harping about me not keeping in touch with him, about not telling him where I was. You know how it went. After a while, it just felt right to cut all ties with you guys. If I continued to keep in touch, Emma would tell Steve where I was. She was always the weakest of us."

Christ, Mary thought. Steve wasn't just on the rebound, as she surmised when he seduced Emma. He was a rejected man, discarded by the woman he'd proposed to. Emma could never know, not in her state. It would break her worse.

"What about after you got married? What's your excuse then?"

"I have no excuse. I just got too wrapped up in my life, my work, achieving my dream, which in retrospect was wrong. I see that now."

"Honesty, that's refreshing from you."

Coco opened her mouth, closed it again when she reasoned she deserved Mary's anger. She hadn't been a friend to her or Emma.

"Emma married Steve." Shock glazing Coco's eyes, she stared at Mary. "How do you feel about that?"

"Sad, I guess."

Mary drew brows together at the comment. "Sad?"

"I didn't know she even liked him."

"Emma fell in love with Steve from the moment she lay eyes on him."

Coco's big green eyes puzzled. "Emma was in love with Steve? Christ, how did I not see it?"

"'Cause, it's always been all about you, and you're blinded to anything going on around you. Emma's always felt guilty about marrying him because of you. The last thing she wanted was to hurt you." Mary watched Coco pick up the discarded toast and absently pick at it. She'd give anything for a cigarette.

"Emma, hurt me, never. She's our buffer, the sweetness between the Oreo."

Mary nodded. "She is." Mary debated whether to say the next words. "I'd like you to stay away from Emma and Steve, for that matter. Steve's still in love with you, and Emma knows it. The last thing she needs right now is to be fraught with additional stress and worry when she and her marriage are hanging by a thin thread." Mary held up an imperious hand to silence Coco when she started to speak. "But I know you won't listen to me. So, if you do look Emma up, keep in mind she's hurting. For once, think of her, not yourself."

"That's our Mary, direct and to the point."

"I mean it, Coco."

Coco got to her feet. "Let's go meet this husband of yours."

Chapter 41

COCO PAUSED AND took a breath when she spotted Emma behind the Xpress checkout. She watched Emma mindlessly scanning Mr. Cole's groceries while he argued with Mrs. Steen that his six packages of spaghetti counted as one item. As vocal as the two were, they didn't seem to exist for Emma, who looked as detached and indifferent as Mary described her.

Tears stung the back of Coco's eyes to see sweet Emma so beaten and unhappy. Coco chastised herself for tossing Mary's sealed letters into the trash. Had she read them, she would have— Coco wasn't sure what she would have done. One thing Coco knew was that Emma didn't deserve what life had thrown her way. It wasn't fair.

She could only imagine the pain and feeling of inadequacy Emma felt as a woman. To learn she couldn't perform the one function her body was anatomically built to do would devastate someone like Emma. Children and a family were all Emma wanted.

Life wasn't fair.

When Mary told Coco Emma married Steve, it pleased her. She never loved Steve, as he deserved, as he wanted her to. He was a void-filler, a lover that satisfied her physical needs. That's all he was. Steve deserved a woman who'd give him as much love as he gave. If that was Emma, then so be it.

That Emma had been in love with Steve surprised Coco. She'd failed to see it because, as Mary said, she was a self-centred bitch. Coco hated it when Mary was right.

Her eyes shaded behind a pair of Dior sunglasses, a hoodie cloaking her face to remain unrecognizable from the public, Coco walked into the store. Picking up a basket, Coco made her way down the aisles. She tossed in shortbread cookies, chocolate ice cream, bananas and grapes, all of Carlo's favourites. Coco threw in a six-pack of Vanilla Ensure as a backup. It was getting more difficult for Carlo to keep solid food down.

Her shopping finished, Coco lined up at the Xpress register. Fourth in line, she nervously waited her turn. As she got closer to the front, Coco felt her stomach knot tighter and tighter.

Swallowing hard, Coco imagined their encounter. What would Emma do? What would she say to Emma? What would Emma say to her?

"Did you find everything you were looking for, ma'am?" Emma asked without looking up from her cash register.

"I have now." Coco's familiar voice drew Emma's gaze.

Looking up to Coco, Emma's eyes rounded wide. "Oh, my God, Coco, it's you. It's so great to see you. I've missed you so much. Where have you been? It's been twelve years since you left." Rounding the counter, Emma took Coco into a tight embrace.

After a long while, she pulled away from the embrace to look Coco in the eye. "Are you back to take Steve from me as you take everything you want? You can't have him, Coco. He's my husband. I want you gone."

That's how Coco saw the conversation going until Emma called out, "Next, please."

"Think of her, not yourself." Mary's voice rang in Coco's head. Fearful she wouldn't be able to steer from the woman she was, apprehension turned into outright panic. Coco dropped her basket and made a mad dash out of the store.

Blindly, Coco ran out of the front doors across the front of the store to the parking lot. In her confused state, she didn't remember where she'd parked her car. Aimlessly she wound her way through parked cars. She didn't remember seeing so many.

Coco looked to her right and her left. Christ, did someone steal her car? She wasn't driving her cherry-red Ferrari. Why would anyone want her crappy rental?

Now a different type of panic set in, and she sprinted forward. She didn't see the man exiting the silver minivan and plowed into him.

"Are you all right?" he said when he caught his breath.

"Yes, I'm fine. Are you okay?" Angling her head, she looked into his eyes. "I'm sorry I wasn't…."

He was older. His dark hair was now dashingly graying at the temples. His tanned face from working outdoors was more handsome with the lines and crevices etched by time. Coco felt a moment's shock. Alarm quickly followed and locked every muscle in her body. Her feet cemented in place.

"I'm fine." He couldn't see the face shielded with dark sunglasses and a hoodie, but there was something familiar about her. The fragrance pumping off her skin, her voice left him digging into his memory.

"Good." Coco heard her heart throbbing, echoing in her ears. She had to get away. "If you'll excuse me."

That voice. He knew that voice. It didn't take long for the connection to follow. After all these years, she came home.

"Coco?" he said.

"No. You have the wrong person." She turned, looked for her car. Where in this parking lot hell was her car?

Steve followed her with his eyes when she darted away. There was no doubt the sensual swing of her gait as she wound through parked cars was Coco's. It was her.

The woman walking away from him was Coco.

The exciting feeling in Steve intensified, and he forgot he was there to talk Emma into coming home. Steve missed Emma. After eleven years of marriage, he'd become accustomed to her presence and her scent. The house felt empty without her. Deciding he'd given Emma enough recovery time after the loss of their daughter, he hoped to talk her into coming home.

Right now, all that went by the wayside. His priority was to chase after the woman he was sure was Coco.

Four cars down, he caught up to her and said, "It's you, Coco. I know it's you."

"Leave me alone, or I'll scream," Coco warned when he refused to move out of her way.

What if Emma came out and saw them together? Coco had to get away, but Steve blocked her way.

"It's you. I'd know you anywhere." He stepped forward. She stepped back, causing her to be pinned between the minivan and him.

Face to face, Coco's heartbeat quickened. She could feel it thumping in her chest. "Get away from me, or I'll scream rape." That made Steve step aside.

"I know it's you, Coco. I just want to talk."

Saying nothing, she rounded the minivan and continued on her way. Steve followed her.

"You disappeared without a word. You owe me that much."

Coco increased her pace while scanning the parking lot. Where was that goddamn car? What was she even driving? She couldn't remember anymore.

"I know behind those sunglasses and that hoodie it's you, Coco. Please. Please don't go."

Heaving a sigh that sounded like regret, Coco stopped and turned to him. Sliding her glasses off, the rich green eyes he knew well stared back at him. "Hello, Steve."

"It is you." Steve's cheeks flushed with pleasure. He wanted to touch her but refrained for fear she'd run away again. "You've come back."

"Not for the reason you think." Coco slid her glasses back on when the two women pushing their shopping cart past them looked over. "I need to get away from here, out of people's line of sight. I don't want to be recognized."

It took Steve a split second to say, "Sure, we can go to the old hangout. It's discreet and private." His hand clamped down on her arm when he thought she was searching for the words to turn him down. "We can share a pizza and talk. Just talk."

"No, not there. I'll drive us in my car to the church parking lot."

His face went brilliant with pleasure at the thought Coco didn't trust herself with him at the motel. "Coco, we're not kids anymore, and this isn't Los Angeles. It's cold here in October, or have you forgotten. Pizza and talk. That's all."

COCO PARKED HER CAR IN THE back parking lot of the motel, away from the main road, and waited for Steve to check them into one of the rooms facing the ravine. Discretion and secrecy were essential to avoid the paparazzi and fans, she told Steve, omitting to mention it was for Carlo's sake. Ever loyal, Steve willingly abided by her request.

"Gianni's Pizza okay with you, or would you prefer Chinese?" Steve tossed his green bomber jacket onto the queen bed.

He wore faded jeans and a black T-shirt. He smelled of the Polo aftershave Coco got him hooked on in their teens. It lit a fire in Coco's stomach. She felt her desire for him flood her body.

Christ, what was she thinking? But it had been so long since she'd been with a man who knew her. A man who knew her body and how to please her as well as Steve did physically.

Coco hadn't gone without sexual gratification during her marriage, but they'd been "encounters" based on contractual agreements. NDAs to keep her sex life, which didn't involve Carlo, secreted was what her life became.

Being there with Steve, the need and want to be loved and be desired by a man who wanted her and not for the generous payout took over and clouded Coco's logic.

She should have gone with her initial gut instinct and avoided being alone with Steve in the motel room, their old hangout nonetheless.

What was she thinking?

Coco reached for the door handle. "I'm sorry, Steve, but this was a bad idea."

Steve's hand closed over Coco's on the handle. "Please don't go."

Coco felt his warm breath on the back of her neck. The blood roared in her brain. "I...." Her voice trailed into a soft moan when she felt the lazy line of kisses down her neck.

Her reaction didn't disappoint. "I've missed you so much." Steve ran a finger up and down her arms.

Coco felt her knees buckle. Think of Emma, Coco told herself. She had to get away from him.

"I really should go." She pulled free from his chained arms.

"I don't want you to go, and I know that you don't want to either." The sexual tension between them that crackled in the air as it always did told him all he needed to know.

"I need to go." Mary's voice harped in Coco's head. Think of her, not yourself.

Steve spun Coco to face him. Before she got another word out, his mouth came down on hers. For a moment, Coco held stiff against him. That is until the greed in his kiss matched his desire for her, and a strong spear of lust that made her hot and wet took over all rational thought.

Falling into the kiss with him, she found his tongue, tangled it with hers in their familiar dance.

The comforting familiarity conjured up so many pleasant thoughts. It made Coco think of their passionate trysts. To have his mouth and hands on her deprived body was strong. She needed this, wanted it so badly, but she pulled away.

"I can't, Steve. This is wrong."

"I've missed you, Coco." Steve's voice was thick and guttural with desire.

His eyes on hers made her melt in his arms just as he wanted her to. Swooping her off her feet, Steve carried her to the bed.

Before Coco knew it, Steve stripped her and himself of their clothes.

She eyed the muscular arms, the broad shoulders. He had aged well, she thought. His chest was firm, his skin smooth. He looked as good as she remembered and exuded the same smouldering sexually he had all those years ago.

The liquid heat spread to her belly. The thrill of feeling him inside her intensified, and she opened up to him, but she knew he wouldn't, not until he tended to her needs. It was who Steve was.

She felt his greedy mouth latch onto her breast like a vice. He suckled until he drove her body to throb with need.

"You're ready for me, aren't you?" he whispered.

Her mind floating, all she could say was, "Mmm-hmm."

"Not yet." He glided his lips along the curves of her body. "I need the taste of you in me."

Sliding his tongue between her legs, he heard her breath catch before she let out an orgasmic moan. It was music to his ears. He lingered, driving her to madness until she erupted.

She didn't sing his name, but she would, Steve told himself. And she did when the next glorious orgasm detonated in her.

Now he was on top of her. Eye to eye and mouth to mouth, he thrust himself hard and deep and hammered the wondrous waves of pleasure through her system until their bodies shuddered to orgasm, and he filled her.

COCO WATCHED STEVE PUSH OUT OF the bed. With the familiarity they'd shared years ago, he walked his naked body to the round table by the window. Steve reached into Coco's purse for the pack of cigarettes. Picking up the ashtray and the complimentary motel matches, he walked them back to her.

"You don't smoke anymore," she said, touching match to cigarette and sucking it to life.

"Em… I quit a while back. Are you hungry? I can order that pizza I promised."

"I'm good, thanks." Coco sighed out smoke.

The trite conversation was the best they could do after the intimacy they'd shared, he thought.

He sat at the edge of the bed, pinned her between his arms. "I've missed this. I've missed you."

"Not now, Steve." She turned her face sideways when he leaned in to kiss her.

The injured expression clear on his face, he rose. "I'm going to grab a quick shower."

Through the haze of smoke, Coco watched him make his way to the bathroom. She told herself what happened was a momentary lapse of control and common sense. It was nothing more than a reaction to the physical stimuli she hadn't felt in so long. There was no emotion involved, none at all.

As true as that was, she knew it wouldn't be the last time. Steve was the only one who could give her what she needed now.

Chapter 42

A DAZZLING, CRYSTAL clear night sky glowed with moonlight and the celestial star streaking across on the cool fall night Carlo died in Alex's arms. Coco, Mary, and Adam stood at the foot of the bed, somberly watching as Carlo took his last breath.

As per Carlo's request, he was cremated and his ashes buried in an undisclosed location. Leaving no trace of Carlo's body for the conspiracy theorists was essential to his legacy.

Coco put out the following press release to announce Carlo's passing on the day of his death.

> My heart is broken today. Carlo, the love of my life, my best friend, my leading man died in my arms today after suffering a heart attack.
>
> To the many fans who expressed concern after he and I disappeared, I offer my heartfelt apologies for leaving you in the dark all these months. The doctor ordered Carlo to take a step back from his hectic life to help his heart heal. Carlo hated being away from all of you and keeping you in the dark, but rest was vital to his health.
>
> I appreciate your support and love and ask that you allow our families and me to grieve in private during this difficult time.

Love, Coco

Heartfelt condolences, flowers, and notes from celebrities, dignitaries, and those in the film industry flooded their Malibu home. A wall of flowers, erected by loyal fans and the many Carlo helped achieve their dreams, appeared overnight outside their homes worldwide.

Admired and loved was Carlo's legacy, and it would remain as such for all eternity. Coco made sure of that.

"IF YOU WANT CARLO'S LEGACY TO persist unscathed, you'll disappear, Coco," said Mary, hot rage burning on top of cold fury.

Coco reached for the cigarette pack on the kitchen table, set them back down when Mary's brow shot up. "What are you saying? Why are you so angry, Mary?"

Mary tossed the pack of matches on the table. "I found them in the living room. They're from the Hampton Motel. Isn't that yours and Steve's lascivious hangout?" The flush of shame whipped colour into Coco's cheeks, and Mary's expression hardened. "Christ, I'd hoped I was wrong."

Coco opened her mouth to deny the allegation but closed it when she figured Mary might have gone as far as to follow her to the motel.

"How long have you been sleeping with Steve?" Mary held a hand up. "Wait, no, I don't want to know. How could you?" Agitated, Mary paced Coco's kitchen.

"I...."

"That wasn't a question as much as an accusation. I realize Steve is as much to blame as you, but he's a man, simple to manipulate with sex, especially by someone like you. You're supposed to be Emma's friend, for Christ's sake. And by your own admission, you have no feelings for Steve."

"I'm sorry," Coco whispered, with an undertone of shame and regret.

Mary snorted derisively. "Yea, that's going to make it all better." She stalked the room as she thought through what to do.

Right now, Mary had to address Coco's deficient sense of judgement. A leopard never changes its spots, whatever possessed her to think Coco would.

"I won't say a word to Emma," Marry offered after a short silence. "I don't ever want Emma to find out about your betrayal. She's too fragile and has enough to deal with without you piling on your narcissistic shit."

"Thank you."

"I'm doing it for Emma, not you. You will always be a selfish bitch," Mary snapped. "I want you to leave, disappear from our lives."

Coco felt a moment's shock at the unexpected request. She was home. Carlo had said just that to her when he turned over the keys to the ten-acre piece of land he bought for her weeks before his death. She planned to make herself at home there, and it was where she and Alex agreed to bury Carlo's ashes. Away from the limelight of Hollywood, away from prying eyes, was where Carlo deserved to rest undisturbed.

"If you don't leave, Coco, I'll make Carlo's true cause of death public," Mary warned when she saw Coco deliberating.

That got Coco's attention. "You wouldn't."

Glaring eyes stared back. "Try me."

"You have an ethical obligation to maintain patient confidentiality."

"Haven't you learned anything from your PR stunts of how information is leaked and facts distorted?" Mary gave Coco a scorching look that said she meant every word. "You look after your friend, and I look after mine. Tit for tat is what you seem to understand, so there it is in a nutshell. I'm losing a good friend because of you. I can't lie to Emma, and putting distance from her is the only way I'll be able to deal with this. So, I'll be leaving too."

The entire conversation felt surreal, but Coco had to focus on someone other than herself for once. Carlo was Coco's priority. She had no option but to succumb to Mary's demand.

Part III

The End

Now and then, your life becomes a poorly directed movie, and only you can alter its outcome.

—M.L. Lexi

Chapter 43

Fall 2002

HER MIND RACING, her nerves bouncing, Mary paced at Coco's front door to calm herself. No good would come of confronting Coco in her agitated state.

What was Adam doing at Coco's home? He never mentioned the visit when they spoke last night. He'd told Mary his schedule for the next few days was jammed-packed with patients. He said he'd be spending most of his time at the hospital. Yet, here he was in the late morning hour at Coco's cottage.

Mary launched into the calm breathing exercises she taught her patients when they became overly emotional. It didn't help, and Mary's mind went where it shouldn't.

Adam was hiding something from her, she told herself. Had Adam become Steve's replacement? Mary wouldn't put it past Coco to seduce Adam.

Casting her mind back, Mary could see now how Coco ogled Adam during his visits with Carlo. Thinking back, Coco always made sure she was in the room when Adam treated Carlo.

And no, she wasn't letting emotion take over. She wasn't letting jealousy read more than she should, Mary told herself. She wasn't the jealous type. She saw what she saw.

The bitch had been seducing Adam the entire time.

Mary supposed her threat to make Carlo's illness public if Coco didn't disappear prodded her to seduce Adam. Tit for tat was Coco's way.

Well, Coco wasn't the only one who could play that game.

Mary's response was immediate, without thought or consideration. "Coco slept with Steve when the two of you were on a break," Mary said and immediately regretted it.

Emma's eyes popped wide. "What are you talking about? Coco was never in town."

Out there, now, Mary couldn't take back what she said, and she told Emma everything. When Mary was done with the surreal account of Coco's sudden appearance, Carlo's illness, and her ultimate betrayal, Emma felt as if she was suspended in a horrible dream.

Emma's face held just enough shock. "No. No, I don't believe it. I don't believe any of it. Coco would have looked me up if she came back."

Mary dropped down on the stone steps and rested her head on her updrawn knees. "I'm sorry, Emma. Everything I told you is the truth."

Emma stared at Mary, and her eyes filled up. Dizzy with pain, without saying a word, Emma put distance between her and Mary. She needed time to think.

Her two best friends betrayed her. They were each complicit in different ways, but both were nonetheless complicit. Mary never told her the truth, and Coco, aside from never showing her face after so many years of absence from her life, took Steve, her husband, to her bed.

Emma went back to Steve after months of therapy. She hadn't known what pain was until she was told she'd never be able to have children. At the news, Emma's world lurched into a darkness she didn't know how to escape.

Emma had to learn how to deal with pain and guilt. She was infertile and couldn't give Steve the children he wanted.

Then, life dealt Emma a great hand and brought a beautiful baby girl into her life. But as quickly as Charlie came, she was taken from her. The pain of losing Charlie was more than Emma could bear. She had to grieve all over again. So did Steve—or so he told her—and at his urging, she returned home.

What was Emma to think now? Did Steve want her back home out of guilt and not because he missed her?

Christ, how could he make love with her after sharing Coco's bed? Emma's spine stiffened, her stomach pitched and rolled.

Maybe she was partly to blame for Steve's pursuit of Coco. Perhaps, Steve hadn't been able to shed Coco from his system because of her duplicity. Making herself look like Coco by wearing the gray-silver wig, the long lashes, and thick makeup to seduce Steve might not have been the best idea. Emma saw that now. Looking like Coco to make Steve love her kept her alive in his mind.

That was her mistake, and Emma would own it, but how could Coco do this to her? Coco's suffering was no excuse to seduce *her* husband.

Betrayed by everyone she loved, Emma had never felt more alone.

Despite Emma's emotional numbness, she felt something after all. Anger propelling Emma, she sprinted across the driveway, bypassed Mary sitting on the porch steps and went straight for the front door. With the strength fueled by betrayal, Emma pushed the oak door open. Finding it open, she stormed in with the breath of dragons.

"Wait, Emma." Bolting to her feet, Mary tried to keep up with Emma. "You need to calm down before you do this."

With the torrent of conflicting emotions swirling in her, Emma raced from room to room. She didn't politely call out to Coco as meek Emma would but demanded she show herself.

Emma wanted to be heard, and today meek, loyal Emma would be. "Where are you, Coco, you betraying, cheating bitch?

"Emma, stop a minute. Breathe," Mary urged.

"I need to find her while I have this mad going. The bitch is going to hear what I have to say," Emma snapped with a fierceness that stunned Mary.

"Emma, you have to calm down."

"She's with your husband." Emma reminded Mary.

That got Mary fired up. She darted up the stairs, taking two steps at a time, and Emma followed.

Going from room to room, Mary threw the doors open. It wasn't until they reached the master bedroom at the end of the hallway they found Coco.

A wave of nausea swept through Mary when she saw Coco in Adam's arms as he tenderly lay her down in bed.

Chapter 44

VISIBLY SHOCKED BY Mary and Emma's sudden appearance, Adam's entire face changed.

"What the hell are you doing, Adam?" Mary's eyes burned fiercely and furious. Adam had never been the recipient of Mary's true wrath. Today that changed. The lava-hot anger pouring out of Mary at that moment was aimed at Adam, and there was a lot more in store.

"It's not what you think, honey," said Adam, reading his wife's mind.

"Don't honey me. I want an explanation of what you and this harlot...." Mary exhaled. "Explain yourself. What is this? I'm waiting, Adam." Mary's foot stomped in anger.

"Mary, you're embarrassing yourself. Don't say another word you're going to regret. Have a seat." Adam's tone was calm.

"I don't want to goddamn sit, and I'll say whatever I damn well want." Mary batted Emma's hand away when she reached out for hers. "I want an explanation, Adam."

Adam opened his mouth to say something, but Coco held up a hand.

Before Coco got a word out, Mary said, "I don't want to hear you, Coco. I'm speaking to my husband. Don't look at her for the script," Mary snapped at Adam when he looked over at Coco.

"Coco's my patient," Adam revealed when Coco gave him the subtle nod of consent.

Mary and Emma looked at Adam questioningly as he looked over to Coco one more time.

"Go ahead and tell them." Coco's voice sounded raspy and tired.

"Coco's been my patient for months now. She came to me, asking for my help when she was diagnosed."

Mary gave Adam a cagey stare out of dark eyes. "Diagnose with what?"

"A glioblastoma. Twelve months ago." Adam's thick eyebrows raised evenly.

Struggling to process the information, Mary studied Adam's face in silence as if trying to determine his story's veracity.

"What's that, Mary? What's a blast? What is it?" Emma pressed at Mary's stunned look.

Adam turned toward Emma when Mary remained silent. "Glioblastoma, Emma. It's an inoperable brain tumour with a survival time of twelve to eighteen months."

The distress flew into Emma's eyes. "Jesus."

"She called me this morning. She had a relapse, and I'm here to look her over." Adam raised the bedcover to Coco's waist.

Digesting the bombshell lobbed at them, there were so many questions—too many to ask—but both were mum. For the longest time, Mary and Emma stared at Coco in dazed silence.

Anger waning to sympathy, Emma crossed to Coco's bed. "You're going to be okay."

Mary held Adam's gaze for a few moments. Adam's subtle shake confirmed Mary's assumption. The anger warring with bitterness in Mary for Coco faded into compassion.

"She's going to be okay, right, Adam?" Emma asked with hopeful eyes.

Coco patted the edge of her bed, and Emma sat. "I'm not going to be okay, Emma."

"What are you saying, Coco." Emma was becoming agitated.

"It's the reason I brought us together this weekend. I don't have long, and I wanted to apologize for what I've done to you and Mary." Coco sucked in a breath when the pain seared her temple.

Emma reached for the glass of water on the night table and brought it to Coco's lips. "Catch your breath, Coco. Relax. You don't have to say anything."

Coco shook her head when the pain dulled. "No, Emma, I need to say this. I'm sorry for not being a friend to you and Mary. Both of you are the best friends I ever had, and I took your friendship for granted. I did things I shouldn't have, and for that, I am so sorry. I know an apology is not much, but all I can do now is apologize."

Another shock of pain lanced through Coco, and she closed her eyes for a moment.

"Are you okay, Coco?" Emma laid a hand on Coco's, held it.

"I am. I sometimes need...." Coco looked up to Emma, sweet, thoughtful, Emma. "I'm sorry, Emma, for what I did to you. I'm guessing from the anger I saw on your face when you walked in, Mary told you."

Emma's reaction was swift as everyone's eyes in the room landed on her. They all knew, down to Adam, they all knew, and no one told her. Bolting to her feet, Emma sucked in a breath and walked to the window, giving them her back.

"Don't be angry with Mary, Emma. She stood up to me for you. She threatened to reveal all my secrets if I didn't disappear. That wasn't easy for her. Telling my secret to the world meant she risked losing her medical license, which is everything to her. She did what she did out of love for you, Emma. Mary is a true friend."

Adam handed Coco three pills and a glass of water. "They will ease the pain."

"But you didn't leave town, did you?" Mary said.

Coco turned to Mary, shook her head. "Before Carlo died, he bought me this property. He told me I was home, where I belonged, where I should make my home. It took me some time to realize he was right and that the only thing driving me was the pursuit of a career that hadn't netted me true happiness." Coco forced the third pill down her narrow throat when Adam prodded her to take it.

"I've made more money than I could dream of, took my career to unimaginable heights, but none of it fulfilled me. Not really. And so, I moved here and built my home. The population of the town is small enough that they'd allow me to disappear in their midst. I'm known here as Jane Smith, my very generic name."

"A few years after settling in, I got antsy and decided to build the spa. I needed the help of the town's residents. My spa was built as a sanctuary for those too well known to hide from the public eye. They come here to get away from the flashes, the reporters, and the paparazzi. Privacy, seclusion is what they seek from me, and it's what I give them. The press can make your career, but it can break you." A breath hissed out between Coco's teeth.

Coco relaxed when Adam wrapped the cuff on her upper arm to take her blood pressure.

"I rounded up the locals and pitched my idea to them. They were more than happy to work with me and maintain discretion. I bring much-needed revenue and work to the town. I've lived here for the past ten years."

"Anyway, back to the reason you're both here. "I'm sorry, Emma, for what I did to you. I know nothing I can say will justify my actions. I was about to lose Carlo, and I felt so lost. I had accomplished my career goals, but I never managed to do the same for my personal life. I needed a … an anchor. I guess that's what you might call it. It was why I got involved with Steve again."

"You couldn't find another man to use for your anchor?" Emma said bitterly when she turned to Coco. "I don't want to hear anymore."

"Hear me out, Emma, please," Coco begged when Emma started to walk out of the room. "It wasn't like that, Emma. All I wanted from Steve was…."

The bedroom door opened, and everyone turned their gaze to Aunt Abby and Fredo trotting close behind. But it was the boy by her side that caught their attention.

"Jesus!" Mary clapped a hand over her mouth.

"This isn't going to be good for anybody," Adam murmured under his breath.

Eyes wide, Emma stared at the boy. She felt the bile rise in her throat. There was no doubting what she saw.

His hair was a thick bounce of dark curls. His eyes were intelligent, and his mouth was wide and generous. He was ten years old, and there was no doubt he was Steve's son.

Emma's heart plummeted to her stomach. Emotion overwhelming Emma, she fought back the tears. Pain and suffering seemed to cling to her.

"Mommy, Mommy," the boy cried out and darted across the room to Coco's side. The dog followed close behind.

"Hi, baby." Coco put on her best face for the child and gave him a noisy kiss on the cheek. "Honey, I would like you to meet Dr. Tyrell and his wife, Dr. Carter."

"Lots of doctors. Aren't you feeling sick again, Mommy?"

Coco curled her fingers into his. "No, I'm fine, baby.

He laid his small hand on Coco's cheek. "I'm a big boy. You can tell me the truth."

The gesture had tears stinging the back of everyone's eyes—including Emma.

"Baby, I want you to meet Emma. Everyone, this is Aiden."

Aiden hopped onto the edge of the bed and prodded Fredo to do the same. "Is she a friend of yours, Mommy?"

"I sure hope so, baby."

Aiden said, "Hello, Emma, it's nice to meet you."

Lowering the hand pressed to her mouth, Emma said, "Hello," as she tried to block off the pain that stung like acid in an open wound.

"Mommy has to talk to these people. Go with Aunt Abby to the kitchen and get a glass of milk and those chocolate chip cookies you like so much and take Fredo with you."

"Okay, Mommy. Come one, Fredo." Aiden hopped off the bed. "Can I have three cookies?"

Coco brushed the hair away from her face. "Sure, but only three, okay?"

"Promise. Can Fredo have a treat too? Please, Mommy. He likes to eat as much as I do. Don't you, boy?" A bark and a doggie grin followed.

"Of course, honey."

Thank you, Mommy." Aiden gave Coco a peck on the cheek before walking toward Aunt Abby.

"What do you say to Mommy's guests?" Aunt Abby said.

"Oh, yeah." Aiden turned to face the group. "Nice to meet you all," he said and walked out the door.

Unable to hold the tears back anymore, Emma ran out the bedroom and out the front door. The tears streaming from her eyes, Emma ran and ran and ran.

Chapter 45

EMMA'S STOMACH RAW, the adrenaline coursing through her veins, like a cloud of storm and fury, Emma ran past the grove of trees that screened Coco's home from the resort. She ran past the lodge, around the stables and paddock. With an awful sour sickness in her stomach and no destination in mind, Emma just ran.

Emma needed to get as far away from everyone.

Seeing Steve's son was a punch to the stomach. The worst part, Emma wasn't sure whether Coco was having an affair with Steve or giving him the son she couldn't, was what hurt most.

Either way, Emma's world crumbled like fine Baccarat into a million pieces. Self-pity, anger, and inadequacy intensified in Emma and propelled her to run faster.

The cool wind on her face, the open green rolling hills calmed her mind. Solitude was underrated, she thought.

As much as Emma wanted to hate Coco, her impending death made it impossible, but she could hate Steve. He betrayed her then slipped into her bed as if nothing had happened.

How could he do that to her?

All Emma ever did was love him. She warmed his bed and kept his home, and that was after ten-hour workdays on her feet. She deserved better from Steve, from Coco, even from Mary, she told herself. Still, she understood that part of the anger pouring out of her was at herself.

She'd stupidly pursued love in a man that had none to give her. No matter how much love Emma had for Steve, his heart belonged to Coco.

There was no changing that. Emma had to let go of everything, and that hurt her.

She was forty-one years old, and all she'd had was heartache. For the remainder of her time on this goddamned earth, she deserved happiness and love to fill her life. And nothing was standing between Emma and the life she wanted except Emma. She realized that now.

There and then, Emma made the difficult decision to leave Steve.

Emma would divorce Steve—and Mary. She would move far away from both to start a new life. This time she wouldn't let the life-gods surprise her. Emma wouldn't wait and hope for the happiness she deserved to come. This time around, she'd pursue it—on her terms. She would shape her life in conformity to her own wants and needs. This time she wouldn't bend her will to the whims of others.

An hour into her run, Emma stopped to catch her breath. Filling her lungs with fresh air, she looked around her. All she saw was a thick carpet of grass, lush and verdant stretching in every direction for miles. There wasn't a road, a house, or signs of civilization. Overhead, wings spread regally, a pair of hawks sailed. Emma heard the wild cry of an animal she couldn't identify and hoped it wasn't close by.

Emma had no idea where she was, and it felt good to be lost.

The pinging message from her cell phone distracted Emma, and she dug into her leggings pocket for her phone. Bringing it to life, Emma saw the many calls and texts from Mary she'd missed. The last text read: Pls, pls, Emma, meet me at the bench under the ash tree. Pls, we need to talk.

Emma's breath hitched. She didn't know what to do.

Emma fell back on the thick grass mat and fell into meditation as taught to her by the yoga instructor. Closing her eyes, with the sound of nature around her, Emma connected with herself for thirty minutes.

Her mind relaxed, and her mental clarity back, she dug out her phone. First, Emma texted Mary to let her know she was on the way back. Second, she programmed the address to the spa. In seconds, her map app pointed her in the direction of the resort.

Chapter 46

MARY WALKED UP to Emma sitting on the bench. Emma's face glowed with a layer of sweat, and there was a rosy pink colour on her cheeks from the run.

"Are you okay, Emma?" Mary held a bottle of water out to her.

"Of course, I'm not okay." Emma ripped the bottle from Mary's hand.

"Where'd you go?" Mary remained standing to give Emma the space she needed. "I've been looking for you for over an hour."

"I started running and didn't stop." I wanted to get away from all of you. "I ended up two miles from the resort."

"You're going to feel that tomorrow. Take a warm bath before bed tonight."

Emma stopped mid-sip and aimed eyes pulsing hot at Mary. "If only you were as helpful when you should have been," she said indignantly.

Mary let the deserved comment pass. The silence lingered for a full minute before Mary said, "Umm, Coco wants to talk to you."

"I don't even want to talk to you, let alone her." Anger didn't look good on Emma. Mary hated herself for inciting it. "I thought you were my friends. I never did anything to either of you."

"No, you didn't. I'm sorry, Emma. I didn't handle the situation well, but I never meant to hurt you."

"And yet you did." Emma's looked at her coolly. "I can never trust you again, Mary. I can't trust Steve or Adam. And I sure as hell can't trust Coco. I can't trust any of the people I love most."

Mary looked down to the ground. "I know I'm sorry, Emma. You really should talk to Coco, Emma."

"All of a sudden, you're an ardent Coco advocate."

"She wants to talk to you about Aiden. I know you're angry, but she's dying, Emma. She has weeks, maybe days. I know you. Even with all the hate and anger, you have toward her, if you don't talk to her now, you'll carry the guilt forever. Talk to Coco. If not for her, do it for yourself."

After a floating silence, Emma said, "All right, but first, I need to shower and change."

Chapter 47

IN THE FOUR poster king-size bed, amongst the multitude of down pillows, Coco looked small but better and more relaxed due to the morphine drip. Aside from the intravenous line hooked up to Coco, Adam and Mary had set up a heart and oxygen monitor.

"Thank you for coming, Emma." Coco's voice sounded surprisingly strong.

"Say what you have to say, Coco." Emma's words came out harsher than she'd intended. "I'm sorry, I didn't mean to sound so harsh."

"You did, and I deserve it," Coco said, aiming eyes over Emma's shoulder to the door when it opened.

At the sight of Steve, Emma shut her eyes, wishing she could disappear in a puff of smoke.

"What are you doing here, Emma?" The surprise in Steve's voice was undeniable.

Emma whirled to Steve. "Don't worry. I'm leaving."

"Don't worry. I'm leaving so you and your lover can have all the time you need." Emma whirled to leave.

"Don't let her go, Steve," Coco called out.

"Coco?" Steve's gaze followed the direction of the voice. That's when he saw her.

She looked gaunt, nothing like the exciting, spirited woman he knew. Alongside the bed, he saw the IV stand and, next to it, the beeping monitors. On the screen, Steve saw the cresting green lines.

Steve's mind raced as tangled thoughts leaped into his head. "What's going on here?"

"I'll explain," said Coco. "But first stop Emma from leaving."

"Don't touch me." Emma yanked her arm from his hold and turned to walk away.

"Please, Emma, don't go. I need to talk to you and Steve," Coco said.

"Why don't you call him what he is? Your lover," Emma said, aiming fiery eyes at Coco then Steve.

"Shit," Steve murmured when the pieces came together in his head.

"Shit, indeed you self-centred, inconsiderate, thoughtless... I'm not going to waste my breath on you. The two of you are made for each other. I can't stand to be in a room with either of you." She paused with a hand on the doorknob. "By the way, Steve, I'm filing the papers for divorce." Throwing the door open, Emma was blocked from leaving by Aiden.

"Hi, Emma."

Emma dropped her gaze to meet Aiden's smiling dark eyes. It was like looking into Steve's eyes. "Hel ... hello," she stammered.

"Me and Fredo are here to visit, Mommy. Isn't that right, Fredo?" The dog barked and raced forward, and Aiden chased after him.

"Christ!" Steve uttered in disbelief. Nothing could have unmanned Steve more than the sight of the young boy who was his mirror image.

Aiden stopped when he saw Steve. "Hello. Are you a friend of Mommy's?" Dumbfounded, Steve could only stare. "I'm Aiden. It's spelled A-I-D-E-N. Not A-I-D-A-

N. Mommy says it's better to be different than common. What's your name?"

"I'm...." Unsure of how to respond, Steve let the sentence hang.

"That's Steve, baby. He's Emma's husband." Coco signalled Aiden to her bed.

"Not for long," Emma murmured, watching Coco frame the child's face with her hands and kiss him on the cheek.

There was love in Coco's eyes for the child, the sort of love a woman who gave life and carried it as part of her being for nine months felt. And the boy loved Coco. That was clear in the emotion that radiated from Aiden's eyes. Coco, the motherly type, wasn't what Emma expected of the woman who'd so often said children weren't a part of her life plan.

"I think it's Fredo's potty time. Why don't you go find Aunt Abby and let her know?"

"I'll take him out. I'm old enough to do it."

Coco ruffled Aiden's hair. "Of course you are, but what have I said?"

"Someone needs to know where we are, always." Aiden recited.

"So, promise me you'll tell Aunt Abby."

Aiden nodded. "Promise, Mommy. Come on, Fredo. I'm taking you potty."

Open-mouthed, Steve watched Aiden chase after the scurrying dog out the door.

"He's ten, and he's your son, Steve," Coco said. Steve's brain felt like it had short-circuited, and he remained silent. "Your name is on the birth certificate." When the silence persisted, Coco went on. "I want you to be a part of his life. I want you to take on the role of his father." Coco flicked her eyes to Emma. "And I want you, Emma, to take on the role of his mother."

As difficult as the words were to say, it brought Coco great relief. She was leaving her son in the care of someone she trusted and lifted a heavy weight off her shoulders.

Coco wasn't ready to die. She wasn't prepared to leave her son, but she couldn't take care of him anymore. She hadn't for months. Nausea and fatigue from lack of sleep, the painful headaches becoming unbearable, made her useless to her boy.

Aunt Abby graciously stepped in to care for Aiden when Coco couldn't, but she was getting on in years and couldn't care for a child so full of energy, curiosity, and self-discovery—as she'd raised Aiden to be.

"I want you to adopt my son and raise him as your own, Emma. I know I can trust you with my son. I know you'll be a perfect mother to him."

Shock robbed Emma of speech, and she said nothing.

"Please say you'll do it, Emma." Flinching at the shooting pain becoming more unbearable, Coco closed her eyes for a moment. When she opened them, Emma was still staring at her. "I know it's a lot to ask and that you need to think it through, but don't take too long. As you know, time is of the essence." Coco gasped, feeling suddenly dizzy. "Oh, God." She sucked in her breath on the sharp pain that suddenly drummed at the base of her skull.

Emma ran to Coco's side. "Are you all right?"

"I need Adam?" Coco murmured.

"Steve, get Adam. He's in the kitchen down the stairs and at the end of down the hallway. Go, go."

Chapter 48

"THAT'S THE ENTIRE story. Leave it to Coco, sorry, Jane," Mary corrected, "to turn her life into a Lifetime movie of the week." Mary set a glass of brandy in front of Emma on the kitchen table and walked the second to Steve at the kitchen island where he sat to give Emma her space. "I thought you'd need it. I'll leave you to it now. I'll go give Adam a hand with Coco, sorry Jane."

For a long while, flabbergasted Steve remained quiet. It was difficult to digest everything Mary told him. When he finally managed to push to his feet, he wandered to the window with a view of the backyard.

Knocking his drink back, Steve watched Aiden chase Fredo, around the yard. The energetic, rambunctious, giggling boy was his son through and through. He'd missed ten years of his life, and he would have missed more if Coco weren't going to— Steve was still trying to come to terms with Coco's prognosis.

As taken aback as he was by Coco's circumstance, her dismissal of his paternity stung deep. He tried to think of a rational explanation for Coco's actions. He couldn't come up with one. She hid his son from him. Emma would never have done that.

It was a stark reality check.

Until today, Steve hadn't realized he couldn't let go of the woman who didn't love him and didn't love the woman who did. For the first time, Steve understood that fully.

How had it taken so long to see what was always right in front of him? How could he have been so stupid? How could he do what he did to Emma? Would she ever forgive him?

One thing Steve was sure of was that he wanted to be a part of Aiden's life.

Steve spun around to face Emma. "I know I've hurt you, and I'm sorry for that, Emma."

"I'm tired of hearing apologies and platitudes." Emma shot back frostily. "Everyone sets out to hurt you and then tries to absolve their guilt with lame-ass apologies."

"You're right." Steve made a concerted effort to speak calmly. "I'm just going to say this, and I'll leave you alone. I want you, Aiden, and me to be a family. I can't do this without you, Emma. I don't want to."

Emma sighed once, then opened her eyes to his pleading eyes. "I can't ever trust you again, Steve."

Emma was defiant, but to Steve's relief, less angry than before. "I know, and I'm...." Steve stopped short of apologizing again when Emma's brow winged. "I want you to be a part of my life, a part of Aiden's life. Choose the future over the past, Emma, and make a life with us. With me. I do love you, Emma." For a beat, he watched her. "It's taken me a long time to say it, but I love you."

The words said with emotion and sincerity caught her by surprise. Her eyes swam when she lifted them to his face. "I've been waiting so long to hear those words? Right now, though, I don't know, Steve."

"Just think about it, Emma. You've been a great wife, friend, and partner. I know you'll be a great mother to

Aiden." Steve left her alone in the kitchen with her thoughts.

This was her only chance to be a mother. A child in her life would heal her broken heart, the pain of loss, and mend the wounds inflicted by Steve and Coco.

It would take a long time to forgive Steve. It might never happen, but it was time to start letting go of the hurt and the anger and the past. By doing so, it would stem the depression that came in waves, ebbed and flowed through her and drowned that temporary ray of sunshine that came her way now and again, Emma reasoned. Life wasn't perfect.

She wouldn't bend her will to the whims of others, especially not Steve, but maybe now, she and Steve with Aiden could find the happiness they both searched for.

The last of Emma's anger melted away.

"COCO'S SUFFERED A GRAND MAL SEIZURE," Mary said, rushing into the kitchen. "Adam's called for an air ambulance to lift her to Mount Sinai. Steve, get Aiden and tell Aunt Abby and my aunt. Have her call Alex while Emma and I throw a few things together for Coco." Mary signalled Emma to follow her.

Chapter 49

EMMA PULLED THE curtains close to block the sunlight bathing Jane Smith's hospital room bright. Adam had registered Coco under her birth name and handpicked the medical staff with her care to ensure her privacy.

"No one deserved to be hounded by reporters in their last hours on this earth," Adam said.

Glancing across at the bed where Jane slept peacefully for the past two hours—with the benefit of morphine— Emma thought how unfair life was. Jane had everything most dreamed of, money, fame, beauty, a wonderful son, and it was being snatched from her at a young age.

Emma couldn't rationalize God's reason for casting such an unfair outcome to befall Jane. As selfish as Jane was, as many mistakes as she'd made, she didn't deserve to have her life taken at such a young age and leave her son motherless.

"Open the curtains, Emma. Let me see the sunshine." Jane aimed groggy eyes out the window when Emma threw the curtain open.

It was a clear sky, infinitely blue and joyful. Jane stared at it with sad eyes.

"How are you feeling? Let me get Adam for you."

Emma started towards the door, stopped when Jane said, "Did you decide, Emma? I know I hurt you and, but I wanted a child so badly. Not just to fill this huge void in my life Carlo was leaving behind, but to make me feel whole as a woman, and I didn't see right from wrong."

Emma met Jane's eyes. For a long silent moment, their eyes held on one another and a moment of complete understanding passed between them.

"I can't undo what I did, Emma. I wish I could. Will you take care of my son for me?"

Emma poured water into a glass and brought the straw to Jane's lips. "Are you asking me to do it because Aiden is Steve's son, and you're hoping he'll be the glue that unites Steve and me after his betrayal? Are you asking me to absolve yourself or out of pity for sad, infertile Emma? I need to know why Jane. Adam registered you as Jane Smith," Emma explained when she read Jane's arched look as one of confusion rather than a reaction to the intensifying pain inside her skull.

"Neither of those reasons. I'm asking you because of the three of us, you're the most maternal and because I've always believed you'd be a great mother," Jane said, not only because she believed it but also because it was what Emma needed to hear. "Will you look after Aiden? Only with him under your care can I rest at peace."

For a long silent moment, their eyes held, a woman who'd tried desperately to have a child faced one who was about to lose hers. It wasn't how it was supposed to be.

Emma's heart deadened with grief. "Of course I will."

"Thank you, Emma. I'm grateful." Jane sat up in bed, wincing at the torturous pain that took hold of her at every move.

"Here, let me." Emma stepped forward, raised the pillow at her back.

Jane reached for Emma's arm. "Promise me, Emma, you'll keep me alive in Aiden, that he'll know who I am."

Fighting back the tears, Emma acquiesced. "Try and stop me."

"I've taped messages for him and wrote a letter for each of his birthdays until twenty-one. I wrote one for when he graduates and marries and has his first child," Jane said bravely.

"I'll make sure he hears every message and reads every letter." Emma wished with every fibre of her being there wasn't a need for the conversation.

"Mommy," Aiden burst into the room on a run. Steve, Aunt Abby, Mrs. Carter, Alex, and Mary walked in seconds after.

Jane's face lit up. "Hi, baby."

"Steve said you may be awake now, and he was right." Steve helped Aiden onto the bed. "We came in a helicopter. It was loud, and it flew really high in the sky. And Steve let me drink a tall carton of chocolate milk. I know I'm not supposed to drink so much chocolate milk, but he said this time it was okay." Aiden set off to recount his adventure with everyone silently listening.

"You've had quite an exciting day. You must be tired."

"I'm not, Mommy. I promise you I'm not."

Jane looked at her son's face, took that picture into her heart, wishing it would stay there forever. "Baby, you know mommy loves you…."

"To the moon and forever," Aiden finished, snuggling closer to his mother.

"To the moon and forever is right, but you know Mommy's not feeling well."

"Mmm-hmm, you told me. It's why you're in the hospital."

"It is, baby."

"But they're going to make you better, right?"

"They've tried, but... Remember the conversation we had about me going away."

Aiden nodded. "You're going to heaven now?"

Emma, Mary, Aunt Abby, Mrs. Carter, and Alex burst into silent tears while Steve somberly watched on.

"I am, baby. While Mommy's gone, I want you to live with Emma and Steve."

"But I want to live with you," Aiden whispered in Jane's ear so as not to hurt Emma and Steve's feelings.

"I know you do, baby, but I won't be here to take care of you, and they want so much for you to be a part of their family. Will you go live with them? Will you do that for me? Please."

"If you want me to, Mommy, I will." He pressed his face to her chest, and she wrapped an arm around him, held him tightly.

"I'm so proud of you, baby. You're the best thing that ever happened to me. The best moments in my life have come since you came into it." The ringing noise in Jane's head was becoming louder.

Aiden pulled back to look into her eyes. "I wish I could go with you."

Jane drew him close to her and laid a gentle kiss on his head. "We'll see each other again one day. Until then, I don't want you to be sad. I want you to be a little boy and do what little boys do. I want you to grow up and fall in love, marry, and have your own children to love as much as I love you. Mostly, I want you to love life." Jane's heart ached at the thought she would never share such simple moments with him or make their own memories. "Will you do that for me?" Jane's arms around Aiden were warm, and he snuggled closer to her.

"I will, Mommy." Aiden rested his head to her chest and started to doze off. "I love you to the moon and forever."

Her heart expanded with a love that knew no bounds. "I love you to the moon and forever," Jane said in a shaky whisper. She hoped he was able to feel her love and that he'd carry it with him for the rest of his life.

The pain came, waves of it, sharp and burning and Jane breathed deep. Mary's eyes darted to the monitor. She didn't like what she saw and, reaching into her jeans pocket for her phone, texted Adam to get to Jane's room STAT.

Mary propped the stethoscope in her ears and walked over to the bed. As she was about to press it to Jane's chest, Jane gave her a subtle shake of the head.

Jane was ready to turn off the unbearable pain forever.

In seconds the darkness came.

No breath.

Holding her sleeping son in her arms, stillness and peace washed over Jane.

The beeping on the heart monitor stopped.

So much stirred in everyone at the sight of the boy snuggled against his mother's lifeless body.

Emma clapped a hand over her mouth as she fought down the wave of sadness that struck her. Her heart wept for Aiden, for Jane, and for her. She lost her best friend.

Aunt Abby fell into Alex, and in the circle of his arms, wept. Mrs. Carter and Mary held one another and cried solemn tears.

Staring at his son in his mother's arms, Steve felt something inside of him break something he knew would never heal. His fatherly instinct took over, and he moved to lift his sleeping son off the bed and snuggled him in his arms.

Chapter 50

THE LATE MORNING sky was lapis blue. The sun was a bright yellow orb. A soft wind rustled through the remaining leaves on the trees, and birds joined in the chorus of birdsong. An eagle soared, and tranquillity reigned over the land.

Under the ash tree, Aunt Abby, Mrs. Carter, Mary, Adam, Fredo sitting on his rump, and Aiden holding Steve and Emma's hand watched Alex set Jane's urn next to Carlo. Smoothing the shovelled dirt, Alex lay a fresh patch of green sod. Coco's burial site would remain as anonymous as Carlo's had.

"Go ahead, honey," Emma said and watched Aiden lay the bouquet of calla lilies at the foot of the tree. Then Aiden raised his small hand and waved goodbye.

"Bye, bye, Mommy."

Blinking the moisture from his eyes, Steve walked up to where Aiden stood. "I carved this out for you." Steve held out the plaque. It was simple and understated, and it said, *I LOVE YOU TO THE MOON AND FOREVER, AIDEN.* "I thought you'd like to hang it on the tree."

"Okay, Steve."

Wiping her cheeks dry, Emma knelt so she could be eye to eye with Aiden. "Steve and I thought you'd like to live here so you can be close to your mom and visit her as often as you like. Would you like that?"

"Mmm-hmm. Will Fredo, Aunt Abby, Mrs. Carter, and Alex live here with us too?"

"Fredo's not going anywhere. He loves it here, and he loves you." Steve said.

"And so do Aunt Abby, Mrs. Carter, and Alex. They're staying here with us," Emma said.

Although Emma knew they loved Aiden too much to abandon him when he needed them most, she couldn't have been happier when they agreed to stay on. Aiden needed his family with him and the stability of familiarity, and Aunt Abby, Mrs. Carter, and Alex were it.

"Auntie Mary and Uncle Adam are going to live with us too?" Aiden's eyes went hopeful.

"They have to work in the city, but they don't live far, and they'll visit often. Would you like that?" Emma said, and Aiden nodded.

Emma signalled for everyone to head back to the house. "Now, we're going to head back to the house. Aunt Abby and Alex have arranged for lunch, with hot dogs and French fries, and pizza, all your favourite foods, to celebrate your mommy's life." At that, Fredo dashed off as fast as his short legs allowed. "I guess he's hungry."

"He's always hungry." Aiden's giggle was a wonderful childlike sound that brought joy to a gloomy day. "Pizza is his favourite food, but we can't feed him too much. Otherwise, he'll turn into a big, round sausage. That's what Mommy says."

"She's not wrong there," said Emma.

Steve concurred. "Then we'll have to roll him everywhere."

With a snort of laughter, Aiden reached for Emma and Steve's hands.

The ash tree and sun at their back and their son between them happily prattling about this and that, Emma and Steve made their way back to their new home and new life.

Sometimes life becomes a beautifully directed movie.

Sneak peek at M.L. Lexi's new novel

THE NOBLE WOMAN

Prologue

The Year 1882

AS ROSA GAVE her heart and body to the man she loved, she accepted she would never see him again. Gianni sailed in the morning for France to marry Contessa Beatrice. That the man she loved more than life itself married another out of love for her, she supposed, was some form of consolation.

Unlike Gianni, Rosa was a realist and understood they were from different worlds. The harsh reality that had touched Rosa's life made her see everything in black and white, not through the rosy-coloured glasses Gianni did.

Their families were as different as the sun and moon and clashed like oil and water. His was blue blood through and through. Hers lived off and for the land. There was a line, and Gianni's family would never allow her to cross it. His royal blood would never meld with that of a simple Sicilian farm girl, no matter how fiercely he defied his parents. They would make sure of that.

"I want to make love with you, I do, but this is not a good idea, *amore*?" Gianni said, in the erudite Italian of the aristocrat.

Before he could turn away, she reached for his arm to stop him. "Tonight's our last night together. I'll never see you again, and I want to be with you," Rosa murmured in the farmworker's coarse Italian.

Gianni's shoulder-length black curls spilled over the handsome face with dreamy blue eyes. "Please don't cry, *amore*." He pressed his face to hers and felt her tear land on his cheek.

"You don't have to do this. You shouldn't do this." He brushed the loose strands of hair from her face.

She was so beautiful, he thought, looking into the jade-green eyes set in a delicate face with skin the colour of burnt honey.

"I want to." Rosa looked at him with eyes that held innocence and optimism until he came into her life.

In the silence she left, the sea whispered secrets, and crickets sang a symphony. Soft beams of sunlight seeped through the old deserted house's cracks on the cliff overlooking the Mediterranean Sea. In the flash of white, dust drifted in the air like snowflakes. There was a tattered rug on the wide-planked floor. Walls, once buttery yellow, were washed-out. Frayed lace curtains billowed at the living room window. Colourful bougainvillea dripping from the paint-flaked pergola above them billowed in a soft summer breeze that brought the scents of sea and brine.

It was their secret meeting place where they met under cover of night and spoke of dreams and love.

"As much as it pains me to say, you need to remain true for the … man you will in time … marry." Gianni swallowed the bitter taste of the words. "I don't want to dishonour you."

Here was love, she thought, feeling the deepest sense of intimacy she'd felt for him, due in part to his selflessness, and in part, to the feel of his body pressed to hers. "I never want to forget you. I never want you to forget me."

"I'll never forget you. Nothing and no one will ever stop me from loving you," he vowed, brushing his lips over her mouth. "And I have our memories. They have a physical, almost realistic quality to them. They will be with me forever. And I have the stars," he said, for the nights they were apart, he looked up to see her beautiful face in them.

"Promise me you will never forget me because I will never forget you." Eyes glistening with tears were full of love for him.

"I promise." "You're my one true love. I could never forget you."

"Then love me tonight, Gianni." Her eyes swam when she lifted them to his face.

His heart wept for her for him. "I love you too much to dishonour you, *amore*."

Rosa reached for his hand, brought it to rest on her heart. He felt her heartbeat against his hand and his beat with hers. "I have never needed your love as much as I need it now."

Gianni pulled her closer, let his fingers trail a slow line down the front of her bodice to untie lace. Eyes on her, Gianni slipped the linen dress and chemise away, inch by inch, revealing soft, sensual curves.

His mouth brushed over her shoulders and neck to her lips. Untying the white kerchief around her head, Gianni loosened the long braid and let her dark hair tumble in waves over the milky white shoulders to her breasts.

With one long measuring survey, his eyes took in the long lines, the soft curves. "You are so beautiful. More so than what I had pictured in my fantasies these past six months."

"You thought of me like this?"

"Often. After all, I am a man, but I would never..."

"And I'm a woman." Taking his hands, Rosa pulled Gianni down onto the tattered rug. "Make it special, Gianni. Make it memorable."

Even as he felt something inside him breaking, in the abandoned house where they often hid from the judgemental world that didn't approve of their relationship, Gianni played his mouth over hers. Lingering, he took his time, as much for himself as for her.

His mouth and fingers set off to explore that which would be his only for tonight. He filled her with sensations that set her body aflame and brought her to heights she'd remember forever. Gianni made love with her for the first and the last time.

The pain throbbed in him like a deep, infected wound.

Afterward, her scent, mixed with his floating around them, Gianni held her as the tears flowed down her cheeks. "Please don't cry."

"I don't mean to, but you touching me in this way, I … I never imagine it would feel as wonderful and beautiful. I didn't think I could love you more than I already do."

Gianni's fingers brushed over her tear-stained cheeks. Sensing the struggle brewing inside her, he looked into her eyes. "I'm sorry for hurting you as I am. I don't want you to be sad. I want you to be happy and for your life to be full of love and joy. You must find a man who will do so."

More tears spilled from her wounded eyes. "I love you, Gianni. I love you so much."

Gianni held Rosa as she cried out her sadness until drained and exhausted she slipped into sleep.

Watching Rosa looking peaceful in sleep, Gianni felt so small beside her. He was a coward. He wasn't half the man to the woman she was.

How could he leave her behind to marry another? Rosa was his world, his life, his air. At the thought of the life he was about to embark without her, he felt adrift, anchorless in a deep, dark ocean. Gianni hoped she'd remember tonight with fond affection.

Gianni regretted being who he was. He hated his family for putting Rosa through everything they had. He resented them for hurting her as they had and keeping them apart. As much as he hated to leave her, it was the only way to put things right because staying would cause her more pain.

Grieving for both, Gianni touched his lips to Rosa's, filled himself with her taste, her scent. Crying silent tears, he took her picture into his heart. "You are the best of me. I love you, Rosa. I always will," he whispered, setting the envelope by her side.

His cape swirling in the wind as he galloped off into the shadowed night, Gianni never looked back.

ROSA NEVER SAW OR HEARD FROM Gianni again, but she wouldn't soon forget him, for the contents of the envelope changed her life in unimaginable ways. And unbeknownst to her, it would do the same one hundred years later.

Coming Soon

The Complete Woman
The Conflicted Woman
The Spiteful Woman
The Tortured Woman

The Relentless Woman Duology

The Relentless Woman
The Vindictive Women

The Unbreakable Woman Trilogy

The Unbreakable Woman
The Brave Woman
The Valiant Woman

Contact us

Email us at mllexiauthor@gmail.com to receive emails whenever M.L. Lexi publishes a new book. There is no charge or obligation and your information will remain confidential.

Visit us at www.mllexi.com to read excerpts of upcoming releases.